Storytime Jamboree

Books by Peter J. Dyck

The Great Shalom
Shalom at Last
Storytime Jamboree

A Leap of Faith

With Elfrieda Dyck

Up from the Rubble

Storytime Jamboree

Peter J. Dyck

Illustrated by Sherry Neidigh

HERALD PRESS
Scottdale, Pennsylvania
Waterloo, Ontario

Library of Congress Cataloging-in-Publication Data
Dyck, Peter J., 1914-
    Storytime jamboree / Peter J. Dyck ; illustrated by Sherry Neidigh.
        p.   cm.
    ISBN 0-8361-3667-5 (trade pbk. : permanent paper)
    1. Bible stories—English. 2. Animals in literature.
[1. Bible stories. 2. Animals—Fiction.] I. Neidigh, Sherry, ill.
II. Title.
BS551.2.D93   1994
220.9'505—dc20   93-50209
                                                                CIP
                                                                 AC

The paper used in this publication is recycled and meets the minimum requirements of American National Standard for Information Sciences—Permanence of Paper for Printed Library Materials, ANSI Z39.48-1984.

STORYTIME JAMBOREE
Copyright © 1994 by Herald Press, Scottdale, Pa. 15683
        Published simultaneously in Canada by Herald Press,
        Waterloo, Ont. N2L 6H7. All rights reserved
Library of Congress Catalog Number: 93-50209
International Standard Book Number: 0-8361-3667-5
Printed in the United States of America
Book design by Jim Butti
Cover art by Sherry Neidigh

03 04 02 01 00 99 98 97 96 95 94 10 9 8 7 6 5 4 3 2 1

*To Ruth and Rebecca,
our daughters,
who long ago
got me started
telling stories to children*

Contents

Preface 8

First Day
    Morning: Osi and Bozo 15
    Afternoon: Repairing the Dam 26
    Evening: Fire in His Belly 50
    Bedtime: The Raft 61

Second Day
    Morning: The Big Fight 69
    Afternoon: The Beaver Brothers 85
    Evening: Now Who's the Good Guy? 117
    Bedtime: Burly and Blinky 131

Third Day
    Morning: The Double-yolked Egg 143
    Afternoon: The Squirrel Festival 162
    Evening: Coony, You're a Loony 170
    Bedtime: Questions 180

The Author 183

Preface

Once long ago in a faraway country, the animals met for a three-day jamboree. It all started when Badger and Beaver, two good friends, were talking about their children.

"Last night when I tucked my children into bed, they asked me for a story," said Badger. "I told them about the time when my grandfather Osi dug his first burrow. When he had finished it, some bad guys came and took it away from him. That happened several times. But Grandpa Osi wouldn't fight. He always let them have the burrow."

"Did they like that story?" Beaver wondered.

"Yes, they really liked it, and they asked a lot of questions. But while I was telling the story, something happened to me."

"To you?" Beaver laughed in surprise. "Don't tell me you went to sleep instead of your children?"

"Not at all. Just the opposite. I was suddenly more awake than an owl at midnight. I realized that in our family are many good stories we have never told our children. The thought hit me like a rolling stone: what a shame if they all were lost!"

• • •

That was the beginning of what turned out to be one of the greatest jamborees the animals had ever had. They called it "Storytime Jamboree."

Of course, they did many other things besides tell stories. They played and danced, they swam and ate, and they did a lot of visiting. But storytelling was the most important part of the daily program.

The animals came to share their own stories and to hear the tales of other animals. Every family had different tracks to trace. And they were all true reports.

The badgers and the beavers, the squirrels and the raccoons, the lions and the leopards, the bears and the weasels, yes, even the ducks were there for the big event.

"*We* know what happened long ago," said a sleek weasel, stroking his shiny brown fur. "We are grandparents now, and we have lived a long time. But our children and grandchildren know nothing about our many interesting experiences."

"You're so right," responded Raccoon with a nod and a smile. "And that's why we know who we are. You know exactly who *you* are, and I know who *I* am because of our claws on the past.

"Knowing those stories of yester-moons, we can trot the trail of all the weasels and raccoons that lived before us. But if our children don't know about that, they won't know who *they* are, and they might stumble into a trap."

"That's just the way I see it, too," replied Weasel. "Our children need a stronger sense of ID, identity. The best way to give them that is to tell them what we went through. Sharing our stories with them will—"

Weasel and Raccoon might have gone on talking like that for a long time. But just then they were drowned out by the bell calling all the animals together for the first big open-air session.

First Day

It was a grand sight. The sky was blue with only a few scattered clouds drifting peacefully over the large open space on the edge of the forest. The sparkling lake was further down the slope. Between the forest and the lake, the animals gathered, some in family groups and others mixed.

The youngsters all made their way to the front so that they would be near the storytellers. Everyone sat comfortably on the green grass, covering an area almost the size of a football field. There must have been a thousand or more.

Rabbit, the chairperson, stroked his whiskers as he looked out over the large crowd. He was pleased that so many had come, that the weather was so beautiful, and that they had so many volunteers to tell their stories.

This promised to be a jamboree everyone would remember. With two hops he was up on the trunk of the big tree that had fallen over. When everybody saw him on his platform, they stopped chattering to hear him speak.

"Friends and neighbors of the forest, prairie, lake, and river, I bid you a hearty welcome! This is our first Storytime Jamboree. We are calling it our Storytime Jamboree because every day we are going to hear three stories: one in the morning, one in the afternoon, and another one in the evening.

"I don't need to tell you about the importance of stories, tales of our own past. If we don't know where we come from, we probably won't know where we're going. It's as simple as that.

"Now that brings me to the three basic rules that all of you storytellers must obey:

"First, the stories must be true.

"Second, the stories must make a point, teach a lesson, without beating us over the head.

"Third, all stories must be interesting. Being dull will put us to sleep.

"Brother Badger has agreed to tell us the first story. He has given it a catchy title, 'Osi and Bozo.' Bozo sounds like a bad guy to me, especially if you draw out the z's and say Bozzzo. But we'll see. Let's give Badger a big paw and our full attention."

Badger looked out over the large crowd, cleared his throat, and began to tell his story.

Morning: Badger's Story

Osi and Bozo

This is a story about my grandfather Osi and his first burrow. Only four days after he married my grandmother, he set out to find a suitable place for their new home.

As many of you know, we badgers marry for life. After we have found each other and fallen in love, we never separate. We live together, have children, and work and play together as long as we live. We stay married to the same partner all our life.

So my grandfather Osi was looking for the right spot to dig a burrow where he and his young wife could settle down. Our children stay with us in the home burrow for most of the first year. That meant Grandpa Osi had to dig a fairly big burrow, with lots of rooms, storage space, hallways, tunnels, yes, and even a bathroom.

Now Grandfather Osi didn't have to dig his first burrow all by himself. Some of his brothers came along to help him. They enjoyed working together. We badgers all do.

One day in their third week of digging, they expected to have it finished by afternoon. All morning they had been grubbing dirt, slinging it from one to the other, to get it out of the burrow.

"Let's take one more rest," said Grandpa Osi as he crawled out of the burrow and rolled himself on the green grass. "If this isn't the best life for a badger, then I don't know what is."

His brothers stopped tunneling and joined him on the surface.

"Isn't this sunlight beautiful?" remarked one of them. "So bright and warm."

They all agreed that it felt good to be above ground for a change. They stretched, shook some earth out of their light brown fur, and lay down to rest.

"This is the life," repeated Ozi once more. "When the cold weather comes, the rain and the snow, when the wind starts howling and the snowdrifts pile up, then we'll be in our tunnels and our rooms, snug underground. We won't even mind that they are dark because we'll be dry and safe."

"And happy!" laughed one of his brothers.

"And happy!" echoed Osi, as his brothers gave him a warm smile.

They all agreed they had dug a nearly perfect burrow. So they began chattering about the fun that Osi and his wife were going to have down there in their cozy home, playing games, eating the stored-up food, sleeping long hours, having children, with not a worry in the world.

"Did you say 'not a worry in the world'?" asked Osi? "Look who's coming over that hill!"

Bozo and Osi

All his brothers sat up and stared. They didn't like what they saw. There was Bozo and his longhaired friends. Everyone knew they were a bad lot.

The shorthaired brothers looked at each other and then at Osi. They were uneasy and yet sure that he would know how to handle these hoodlums. He was good at that.

"So you dug yourself a nice home for the winter!" said Bozo, leader of the longhaired badgers, with a sneer. He stepped forward, and the others made a fighting wedge behind him.

As they glowered at their distant cousins, Bozo asked, "Are you finished with the grubbing? Got all the digging done? The rooms and tunnels shaped? Got a second exit for safety, just in case?"

"It's as good as done," answered Osi. "We are just taking our last rest, and then we are going to fetch my new wife."

"How nice!" snarled Bozo in a voice the shorthaired badgers didn't like. "We came at just the right time."

"What do you mean, you 'came at the right time'?" Osi wondered. "The right time for what?"

"The right time to take over the new burrow," boasted Bozo of the longhaired badgers. "You might as well move along right now. Just leave this burrow to us."

Osi was stunned. He couldn't believe his ears. He and his brothers knew that the longhaired badgers had a reputation for being mean and sometimes unfair, but not like this! No way! This was going too far. But he kept his voice down and showed no anger when he responded.

"Do you know how long we have worked on this burrow? For weeks we came here day after day and worked hard. You can see by the size of that pile how much earth we moved. That also gives you an idea how roomy and big this burrow is.

"We scratched and clawed, we shoved and pushed, we threw all that earth out on the surface. And now you say this burrow is yours. It's ours, of course. I hope you were just kidding!"

"All right then," bellowed Bozo. "If you don't give it to us, we'll just have to take it. But we give you fair warning. After we're through with you, you'll crawl away as cripples. Some of you won't even crawl. You'll be meat for the farmer's dogs!"

Turning to his longhaired ruffians, he snapped, "You heard him. It's not our fault when stupid folks get hurt. We asked them decently. Now get ready to attack! I'll count to ten. You all know what to do! One . . . two . . . three—"

"Just a minute!" exclaimed Osi. "Give me a moment to talk it over with my brothers."

They got into a huddle, whispered briefly, and turned back to face the longhaired tough guys.

"That was a misunderstanding," Osi explained. "No problem at all. You can have our burrow. It's yours."

Osi and his brothers moved away. They went clear to the other side of the valley to be out of sight and sound of Bozo and his gang. It didn't take them long to know what they had to do or how to do it.

They began to dig another burrow right away.

Now they had to work faster because much of the summer was over and winter would be coming soon. The newly wedded couple needed a home.

At last the day came when they had the second burrow finished. With all the extra digging experience, they made this one even roomier and nicer than the first one. Like the other time, they all came to the surface for one last rest.

This was a time to chat about the new home, their families, and the children. They dreamed about the good time Osi and his charming wife were going to have down there during the cold and blustery winter.

"Won't she be surprised when she sees how much space it has?" Osi was feeling so happy. "And you have all worked so hard. I thank you all."

"Did you say *surprised?*" asked one of his brothers. "Look who's coming now! We have *another* surprise."

Sure enough, moving toward them along separate paths came two gangs of longhaired badgers. That could only mean one thing: TROUBLE.

They came up to Osi, and this time Bozo, their leader, didn't even bother to ask how they were doing or whether they were finished. He walked right up to Osi and growled, "Thanks. We can use another burrow. So why don't you all just quietly move along? This one belongs to us."

Osi and his brothers were stunned. They hardly knew what to do.

Bozo didn't wait for them to respond. "Scram!" he barked. "The whole lot of you! Unless you'd rather stay and fight."

Osi saw the hairs on their necks and backs rise and bristle. He knew what that meant. He saw the fire in their eyes and heard them snarling.

They were a rough bunch, eager for a scrap. No use arguing with them. They wouldn't listen to reason. They looked as if they would even attack their own mothers. And the shorthaired badgers were only distant cousins.

"We want no bloodshed," declared Osi. "A burrow is valuable property, but it's not worth dying for. We dug it, and it's really ours. But if you want it, you can have it."

Off they went, Osi and his brothers, to find a good spot for their new burrow. They'd have to start digging at once and dig fast because fall had already come.

Never before had they dug one burrow after another. This was their third one. Now they hardly stopped for food and rest. Winter was not far away. They simply had to have a home before the snow came.

Yet they had lots of digging practice, a strong will, and healthy bodies. They actually enjoyed what they were doing, especially since it was teamwork.

When at last their burrow was finished, Osi called his brothers together and spoke in a voice that carried pride and satisfaction. "We did it again! Looking back on the other two burrows, I hope you realize that it was the best thing we could do, letting Bozo and his gang have them."

"You're right," agreed his brothers. "What they did is on their conscience, not on ours."

"That's true," agreed Osi. "Look at it this way: all we really lost was time. We lost no lives, none of us got hurt, and we didn't hurt them. Who knows, maybe someday Bozo and his gang will have a change of heart and become decent badgers."

They lay on the grass, resting and enjoying a bit of fall sunshine. Then Osi had one more thought.

"See that large mound of earth we piled up?"

They couldn't help but see it. It had grown day by day as they chucked more and more earth up from under the ground. So why did he ask?

"You see it, I see it, and everyone else can see it," Osi stated. "I don't need to tell you that we might as well put up a sign saying ENTRANCE TO THE SHORTHAIRED BADGER HOME. Not only will Bozo and his gang know immediately where we are, but every dog and wolf and even the hunters will know exactly where to find us.

"Is that what we want? Traps, guns, and who knows what else at the mouth of our new burrow?"

They all agreed that Osi showed brilliant insight. Without a word of protest, they jumped up and began scattering the earth from the mound.

When it was all thrown far away and Osi was about to fetch his wife, one of his brothers sighed, "Oh no! I don't believe it!"

You guessed it. On the very day they finished their third burrow, the very hour when they had scattered the mound of earth so that they wouldn't be seen so easily, the longhaired badgers were back.

There was no question in the mind of Osi or his brothers what they had come for. Osi's badgers already knew what they themselves would do. They'd let the longhairs have the new burrow and move on to dig another one.

No surprises anymore. This was getting to be routine, a disgusting and discouraging routine. One that they could do without. But better to let them have it than to fight and get hurt, crippled, or killed.

"Well, well, another burrow!" exclaimed the leader of the longhaired badgers as he came closer to Osi and his shorthaired brothers. "You are getting expert in digging burrows. You did this one in record time. And scattered the earth, too."

Osi didn't say anything. He knew what Bozo was going to say next, and there was no point in arguing with him. They certainly were a mean bunch. So he just kept quiet and waited.

"We have watched you carefully," Bozo went on. "You are good workers. But more than that, you are an agreeable lot. It's hard to pick a fight with folks like you."

"We don't think violence is the answer," Osi stated. "Fighting doesn't solve problems; it just makes more problems. We don't intend to hurt you or anyone else."

"So we see," responded Bozo. "As you know, that's not *our* way. However, you made us think. We don't want to hurt you, either. Is there any way we could live together in peace?"

Osi didn't know whether he had heard right. He could hardly believe his ears. Was this a trick?

"You didn't come to take this burrow away from us?" he asked in surprise.

"It's yours," Bozo assured him. "You dug it, you keep it. Live in it, you and your new wife."

"If . . . that's how you . . . feel about it . . . ," stammered Osi at last. He could not understand what had happened nor make a quick response. "If that's how you feel about it, then let me make a proposal."

Thoughts were tumbling wildly through his head. His brothers smiled and nodded their support, whatever it was he was about to say. They had complete trust in Osi.

"I'd like to suggest," he continued, and then corrected himself. "No, this is not just a suggestion but an invitation. I'd like to invite you and your families to join us here tomorrow night with our families for a feast. We would like you to be our guests. We'll make it a real banquet. What do you say? Will you accept?"

"Now if that doesn't beat everything!" replied Bozo. "We take away your burrows, and you invite us to a feast!"

Bozo and his gang accepted gladly. They slapped paws all around, and the next day they had a feast that lasted all night. They ate and drank, they played games and danced, they talked and they hugged each other.

After that, there was peace between the long-haired and the shorthaired badgers.

If you would like to read this story as it was written the first time, take your Bible and turn to Genesis 26:17-31.

The older animals had just gotten up from their afternoon nap when the bell rang for the second session.

"You told a great story this morning," complimented Muskrat as she waddled alongside Badger to the meeting.

Badger grinned. "That was my grandfather. He'd rather dig another burrow than fight for it."

"But don't you think we should talk about the lesson in that story?" Muskrat wondered. "Chairman Rabbit said that every story must make a point. But what if some don't understand?"

"Discussing it is not necessary," replied Badger. "If they didn't get the point when I told the story, I don't think telling them now would help much."

"But the children, do you think they learned anything from it?"

"Children catch a lot. Why don't you go and ask them what they heard me say this morning. I'm sure they'll tell you that they heard a peace story."

Badger and Muskrat had arrived at the place of meeting. Chairman Rabbit was up on the fallen tree again, waving his paws for silence.

"My friends, furry and feathered, we have a real treat in store for us this afternoon. Since Badger and Beaver were the ones to come up with the idea of a Storytime Jamboree, we gave Badger the first chance to tell a story.

"I'm sure you all agree it was well worth hearing. Now we call Beaver to come up here where we can all see him and tell us another story. The title of his story is 'Repairing the Dam.' "

Afternoon: Beaver's Story 1

Repairing the Dam

This is the story about my uncle Haimehen. But actually, the story is much bigger than my uncle. It's a story about our town and our people. A story of harm and hope.

Let me start where things began to turn around. If you listen carefully, it will all become clear.

My uncle Haimehen (Haim for short) had swum as close to the dam as he dared. It was still broad daylight, and he didn't want to risk being seen by anyone.

He swam around quietly in the lake he used to know. Then he decided to wait until dark before inspecting the damage done to the dam. Uncle Haim was excited to be so close to what had once been his home community.

It had been a long journey, and my uncle was tired. Crawling ashore, he shook his brown fur briskly until it was almost dry. Then he stretched out on a bank, making sure he was well hidden by the deep grass. Soon Uncle Haim was asleep.

It was not a good nap. As he tossed, restless, the memories all came back to him: the surprise attack by the enemy . . . the big fight . . . the dam destroyed . . . and most horrid, being dragged away from home to a faraway country.

Haim remembered it all as if it were just yesterday, even though it had happened twenty years ago. The pain was still there. How he loved this place! How he had longed to return!

As he lay there recalling the events of long ago, Haim thought about the news that had trickled to him in that distant land, drop by drop. Back home his people were poor and sad, their city smashed, their dam broken.

These were *his* people. It was *his* city, *his* dam. Without the dam, there could be no city. All the water would run off, so there would be no lake.

Without a lake, there would be no dome-shaped beaver lodges, their homes, sticking up out of the water like little islands. He wondered how much of the dam had really been destroyed.

What about the people? Would they listen to him and his plan? Would the old enemy leave them alone at last?

Uncle Haim had many questions. Yet he never doubted for a moment that the Great Spirit was with him. Sure of that, he rolled over and tried once more to sleep. He needed it. The night would be long and hard.

When he awoke, the moon was high above the trees, and the lake lay shimmering before him. Haim stretched and yawned. A frog croaked near by. An owl hooted from a tree.

It would feel good for him to have a bite to eat, but there was no food. He slid into the water as quietly as a moonbeam and began swimming toward the dam.

Most of the time Uncle Haim swam on the surface, but now and then he ducked under to be sure he was not detected. The watertight valves in his nose and ears opened when he was above the surface and closed when he was below. His strong webbed hind legs moved him along without noise and at great speed.

Everything depended on his first contacts back home. This was Beaverlake, his home community, and soon he would reach Beavercity and check on the damage done to the dam. His heart beat faster, not just from swimming but from the thrill of coming home.

"Pssst!" he heard a sound near him. Haim dived and swam as fast as he could, deep underwater. When he came up at last, everything seemed quiet. He saw nobody. He heard nobody. But he wondered what or who had made that sound. The moon still shone bright on the familiar stretch of water. Yes, this was Beaverlake.

"Pssst! Pssst!" he heard again. This time, instead of diving for cover, Haim looked around to see where that voice had come from. At first he saw nobody, but then he heard it again, "Pssst! Over here!"

Haim veered around to the other side of the lake. There, seen only by a keen beaver eye, was another beaver. He was under water, with only his nose and eyes bulging above the surface.

It was a trick few beavers could do well, but in case of danger or in an emergency, it was a useful skill. Questions flashed through Haim's head: Is he friend or foe? Is he a spy?

Having come safely this far, Haim decided to risk being exposed. He was a good swimmer. If the worst came to the worst, he could probably outswim the other fellow, whoever he was.

Quickly looking around to make sure this stranger was alone, Haim whispered, "Come closer and talk," and after a brief pause, "I come in peace."

Slowly the head of the other beaver emerged on the surface. At that moment, a cloud drifted over the moon and made it hard to see. But Haim thought he recognized the beaver.

"Aren't you Mallushem?" asked Uncle Haim. "Speak to me, and I'll know you by your voice."

"I am Mallushem," replied the other. "And you are Haimehen. Welcome back, my friend! You've been gone a long time."

"A long time indeed," agreed Haim. "Twenty years! Tell me, how are the others that have returned after being scattered? How are those who got to stay here after we lost the big fight? How much damage was actually done to the dam?"

There was a long silence. Mallushem did not speak. Finally he said, "You ask a lot of questions. Why don't you come to my house and hear all the news. I'll invite our old friends, and we'll tell you everything. You will be perfectly safe with me."

That's what Haim did. He entered Mallushem's house by one of the underwater tunnels so he would not be seen. All day he spent at his friend's home, listening to reports.

The longer Haim listened, the sadder he became. The news was not good. The people had lost heart. There was no joy in Beaverlake. Even the children went about with long faces.

Food was scarce. An enemy was always prowling around the edges, ready to strike again if the beaten beavers dared to rebuild.

"But Beavercity, how is Beavercity and the dam?" asked Haim. "When I last saw it, just before they led me away a prisoner, some of the dam had been destroyed. How bad is the damage? Are there plans to repair it?"

All the beavers looked sad and shook their heads. "As soon as it is dark tonight and the moon is up, we will show you," promised Mallushem. "It will be a sorry sight. Nothing but ruins. It'll make you sick.

"Now it is best that you eat and rest. You will need all the strength you can get."

"Thank you, my friends," Haim responded. "I appreciate your help. But let me tell you something that may surprise you and even scare you. I have come back to rebuild the dam. You all must help me. I cannot do it alone."

Haim got no further in his little speech. Several beavers broke in and spoke at once. Some said that was foolish. Others said it was dangerous. They all agreed that it could not be done.

Uncle Haim was silent for a long time. He looked each one of his friends in the eyes. As they looked back, they could see that there was no fear in his eyes. They also saw something else there. What it was became clear when Haim spoke again.

"Yes, it would be foolish, dangerous, and impossible to rebuild the dam if we were to do it alone. But we will not be alone. We have help, huge help, sure help. I would not have come to suggest that we repair the dam and Beavercity without knowing of that help."

"From whom?" asked many voices at the same time. "Who is going to help us? Speak up! Tell us! This is good news!"

"The Great Spirit!" replied Uncle Haim as he slapped his tail on the floor with a mighty whack. "He told me. And I believe him."

There was another long silence. A few heads at last began to nod approval. There was some whispering. Then there were more questions and more discussion. Before they drifted away, they agreed to meet again as soon as the moon was up and they could safely swim to the dam. They were going to let Haim see for himself how hard it would be to rebuild.

Uncle Haim saw the damaged dam. It was worse than anything he expected. He felt like weeping. Then a wave of anger surged into his body. What had they done to deserve this? They had not always been perfect beavers, but—

That is as far as he got in his thinking. The moment he wondered if they deserved such hard times, he calmed down. The anger left him.

He knew that they had not been good. They had brought this trouble on themselves. They had acted foolishly. They had not listened to the Great Spirit, and they had suffered for it. They had been punished.

But now a new day had come. They had turned back from their wrong living. So instead of weeping or showing anger, he called the beavers together and told them of his plan.

"We are going to repair the dam. We'll need all the usual materials for building dams: logs, branches, rocks, leaves, mud, and a lot more. But most of all, we need lots of willing paws to do the difficult job.

"This will take mighty muscles and mountains of material," Haim went on. "It will take tons of time, too. But more than anything else, it will take courage. This is not for the fainthearted.

"There will be hard work, and some will be against the project. We know that before we start. So I ask you, my friends, are you with me? Will you hang together, and will you stick with me no matter what happens?"

They knew that Haim was not finished with his speech. The pause was only for them to catch up with his thinking. They needed that. Some of their heads were spinning.

"I have good news for you. I have said it before, but let me say it again. We are not alone in this big job. The Great Spirit himself is with us. That should make all the difference."

At last everyone thumped their tails and agreed to pitch in and help repair the dam. That would be the first big task. After that, if there was muscle and material left, they were also going to do fix up Beavercity. But without the dam, there would not be much city. They just could not stand for the way things were.

Early the next day, the work began. Some beavers were cutting down logs on the edge of the lake, while others floated them over to the broken-down dam.

One crew gathered rocks to weight down the logs, a group of youngsters picked up branches and twigs to stuff between the logs, and still another team of divers dredged up mud to glue it all together.

Other beavers waiting for more material were amazed to see all the activity. As they watched, they became more excited and eager to work.

Everyone seemed to be in a good mood. The spirit of defeat had been turned around. There was hope again, hope for a better and brighter future.

During this upbeat scene, they heard that Tallabnas the Superbeaver was thumping mad about them rebuilding the dam. At first he just made a joke of it.

"That's the funniest thing I've ever heard," he jeered. "Can those skinny skeletons cut down trees? If they float logs along in the water, how can they steer them right? Do they really think they can lift logs to the top of the dam and make them stay in place?"

One of his helpers standing nearby also scoffed at Haim and his beavers. "If a small fish were to swim up against their dam, it would tumble down. If a turtle would walk on that stupid thing, it would break to pieces. It's weak because they're using some old pieces of the first dam. The whole thing is a joke."

Suddenly the mood of Tallabnas changed. He flew into a rage. He shouted all over the place and said he would see that this nonsense was stopped at once. There would be no more repair of the dam.

"What do they think they're doing?" he growled. "I know rebels when I see them! What they're doing is just that, rebelling against me and my orders. I'll let them know who's in charge around here!"

When the beavers working on the dam heard him ranting, they began to shake in their furs. They knew the terror of Tallabnas. Perhaps it was a mistake that they had listened to Haimehen.

Just then Uncle Haim swam up to them. He had heard the news and came to encourage his friends.

"I have sent a message to Tallabnas the Mighty: 'We are not scared by your words. That's all it is, words! We are going to rebuild the dam, and nobody is going to stop us. So why don't you just go and mind your own business?' "

Haimehen paused a moment and then went on: "I also told Tallabnas, ' Whether you believe it or not, you should know that the Great Spirit himself is with us.' "

Having spoken, Haim turned to help two beaver brothers adjust a heavy log on the dam. That was the signal for all the other beavers to get back to work.

Soon the beavers were true to their name—they worked like beavers. They hardly stopped to eat and sleep. Every day more of them joined in the great task.

So the rebuilding of the dam continued.

One day not long after Tallabnas received that bold message from Haim, he called his people together.

"Those crazy beavers are going right ahead, repairing the dam as if we had not defeated them in battle," he griped. "What's more, they pay no attention to our orders and threats. They ignore us completely."

"Tallabnas is right to be upset about this," replied one of his loyal beavers. "It's an insult. It must be stopped."

"But how?" asked Tallabnas. "How are we going to stop them?"

"With your permission," began one of the counselors to Tallabnas, "I will suggest a way. Let us spread word among them that we are going to attack them again. That will do the trick.

"First, it'll frighten them for sure. Some will be so scared they'll stop working on the dam and swim away.

"Second, it'll divide them. Some will be for building, and others will be for stopping. Such a split will weaken them."

"Excellent! Those are brilliant suggestions," agreed Tallabnas. "If we spread the rumor that we're going to attack again, that will weaken and divide them, and they'll start arguing among themselves. Perhaps they'll even start fighting among themselves. Let them kill each other. Then we don't have to do it."

So Tallabnas sent "moles," his spy beavers who work their mischief on the sly and mostly in the dark, to sneak into Haim's beaver colony. Their job was to spread word about the planned attack.

Later, Haim heard what was being whispered among his beavers. When he saw how frightened they were, he called them together to talk to them.

"Do you remember that before we started to repair the dam, we knew there would be problems? We said it would take courage to go on when trouble started. Well, the trouble has started. So here's my plan."

In a strong voice, Haimehen thanked all of them for working together so well. Then he went on, "Tallabnas is furious. He doesn't know how to stop us.

"So now he is spreading rumors to divide us and weaken us. He thinks we might even start fighting among ourselves.

"But Tallabnas doesn't know how united we are nor how much we want to finish the work we have begun. Most of all, he doesn't know that the Great Spirit is with us. He doesn't want to believe that.

"Let's pay no attention to his threats. Tallabnas is a windbag. Let's get back to the job, but be alert. While you work, always keep looking over your shoulders just to be sure that Tallabnas and his men are not sneaking up on us."

Everybody liked the way Haim saw things. They agreed that it was best to go right on with repairing the dam. Every day they could see progress, and they felt new courage.

So the rebuilding of the dam continued.

For a week or two, there seemed to be no trouble from Tallabnas. All the beavers were able to keep working with great zeal.

Yet one night, after a long and hard day at the dam, several of the leaders came to Haim and asked to talk with him. He could tell by their faces and tone of voice that it was something serious.

"It's too much," began the foreman of the tree-cutters. "The work is too hard. All the beavers are tired. Their chopping teeth are worn down. We can't go on like this."

"On top of that, we're afraid that's just what Tallabnas is waiting for," added the foreman of the log-pushers. "His spies are watching us all the time. He's waiting until we're worn out, and then he'll attack us. We won't have any strength to fight him off."

"They're right," declared the engineer overseeing dam construction. "My beavers are bushed, too. I've been pushing them to their limit day after day.

"They're too tired even to slap their tails on the water to warn us when our enemies come. To keep on like this is asking for trouble."

Haim listened to them all. Often he nodded his head. They were right. As their top leader, it would be foolish for him not to agree to make things better. He knew they were his friends and that they believed in the project as much as he did. Now it was up to him to make their load lighter.

"Let me see if I heard everything right," Haim responded. "First, we have the problem of overwork. We are exhausted. Second, we have the problem of Tallabnas and his gang planning to attack us. We need to solve both problems."

The beavers had been sitting on the shore during this conversation. Then Haim called them to slide into the water, form a circle facing each other, and lift their big flat tails to the surface for balance. They were speaking in low voices.

"Here is what I suggest," began Haim. "From now on, only half the beavers will work at a time. The other half will rest—at the dam, not at home. Without napping, they will relax, maybe just floating around or sitting on a log or on the dam. All the time, they will keep a sharp lookout for Tallabnas and his gang."

"A brilliant idea!" agreed the leaders of the work groups.

"Let's call it the half-and-half plan. Half work and half rest, and we change off every few hours. The half that rests keeps looking out for Tallabnas. If he attacks, they will slap their tails on the water to warn us all."

When they brought the half-and-half suggestion back to the rest of the beavers, they all agreed that it was a fine solution. Their problem was solved once more. And Haim had done it again!

By now, they had been busy for most of a month. The dam was getting higher and stronger every day. The new formula of half-and-half was working out just fine.

Tallabnas knew that he had no chance of attacking them by surprise. Half of the beavers were always on the lookout.

So the rebuilding of the dam continued.

When they were close to being done, the engineer overseeing the dam construction called Haim aside and whispered something into his ear. They both swam off to the edge of the lake and waved for the foremen of the log-pushers, tree-cutters, rock-rollers, branch-gatherers, and mud-dredgers to join them.

"Is it true what I hear?" asked Haim, somewhat alarmed. "It's enough that we have trouble from the outside. Do we now have trouble among ourselves?"

"If we did not speak up about this evil, we would not be your friends or the friends of all those good beavers who work so hard under our direction," replied the foreman of the log-pushers. "We put up with it as long as we could, but now the people are getting so discouraged that something has to be done about it."

"But what is this 'evil' that you talk about? Speak plainly so we can understand," demanded Haim.

The leaders of the various work groups looked at each other, wondering who was going to speak first. At last the foreman of the log-cutters spoke.

"It's a nasty business, that's for sure. Nasty for me to speak about it, but much more nasty for all the beavers being treated so unfairly. It's like this."

With great care and in detail, he told Haim about the rich beavers in Beavercity. They were squeezing the poor beavers to make them give the rich ones extra food and service, even making them their slaves.

"If that's true," Haim stated in alarm, "it's a serious charge. Are you prepared to prove it?"

"Oh, we are, we are," chorused several of the foremen together. "Not only do they act mean to the poor beavers here in Beavercity, but they do the same in all of Beavercountry. They mistreat all the beavers that come here to take their turns building the great dam."

"Tell me more about it," insisted Haim. "Give me some true stories of rich beavers acting mean toward the poor ones. I'll bite a notch on this branch for each report you give me."

"Let me speak," volunteered the foreman of the rock-rollers. "I have some poor beavers in my group. They work hard, and they know we need the dam. They never shirk a duty or miss a day.

"But because they're always on the job and never miss a day, they can't keep up with work at home. Soon their food runs out. Their house needs repair. So what happens? They have to borrow from the rich beavers."

"What's wrong with that?" Haim asked. "Shouldn't they be glad that the rich lend them food and stuff?"

"Yes, of course," put in the foreman of the log-cutters, "but that's just the beginning of the story. After they have borrowed food so their wives and children won't starve, the rich beavers turn around and make our workers repay it double, even triple."

"They do it all the time," added the leader of the branch-gatherers. "If they don't pay it back in a certain time, they increase the amount they have to repay. Then they rough the poor beavers up whenever they have a chance."

"Here we are, all of us working together for the same cause," the chief engineer of the dam construction team summed things up. "In fact, the poor beavers are working much harder than the rich beavers."

"At first we thought we all were brothers and sisters, all working to rebuild the dam, all believing in the Great Spirit. But that's not the way it turned out."

"Enough! Enough!" exclaimed Haim in a stern voice. "I'll do some more checking, and then we'll have an open meeting to settle the matter."

The next day Uncle Haim called for the meeting of everyone. He did not say what it was about. There had been many meetings, so this was not unusual. Most beavers thought it probably had to do with repair of the dam, or perhaps something new about their enemy, Tallabnas and his gang.

They were surprised that Haim asked the rich beavers to come right up front. "Swim real close to me," he encouraged them as they gathered along with the rest of them. "We have important business to take care of."

When the rich beavers heard the word *business*, they perked up their ears. This interested them. They were always ready to do more business, to get more wealth.

For this meeting, Haim skipped any word of

praise or introduction of the matter at hand. He pointed his paw at the rich beavers around him and growled, "What is this that I hear about you?

"How dare you demand more food from the poor beavers than what they borrowed from you in the first place! How dare you use the need of the poor beavers to squeeze them so! Are you not all brothers and sisters? Are you not all working here for the same cause?"

There was uneasy shuffling among the rich beavers. They wished they weren't right up front with everybody watching them.

Haim continued, "These are your brothers and sisters, caught in the big fight and dragged away to a distant country as slaves. So was I.

"Then some of them were allowed to come back to Beavercountry and settle in Beavercity. They were set free from being slaves. But now they have fallen into *your* paws. Now *you* are making them *your* slaves!"

The rich beavers wished Haimehen would stop. It was all true, but they thought he'd gone far enough in telling about their secrets.

"What you are doing is very evil," Uncle Haim declared. "Don't we have enough enemies on the outside? Do you have to destroy us from the inside? Don't you fear the Great Spirit at all?"

Then he made the rich beavers promise to give back to the poor beavers the extra payments, whatever was more than what they had borrowed. Grudgingly they agreed to stop treating the poor beavers unfairly.

Finally Haim declared in a firm and angry

voice, "If you do not keep the promises that you have made here today, may the Great Spirit destroy you and your homes and food supplies, the way you are destroying the poor beavers' homes and food supplies."

After the meeting with the rich beavers, Haim met with the foremen of the various work groups. He was exhausted. Turning to them, he stated, "I hope that problem is settled. Thank you for bringing it to me. Let's see, that was our fourth big problem since we began rebuilding the dam."

"That's right," agreed the construction engineer. "First, there was the threat from Tallabnas when he said we were rebelling against him. Second was the rumor that Tallabnas was going to attack us. Third was the problem of overwork and lack of protection from enemy attacks. And now, fourth, this problem with the rich beavers not being fair to the poor beavers."

"I feel like saying, 'Enough is enough!' " exclaimed Haim. "But the dam is not yet rebuilt, and we'd better be prepared for more trouble. We all agreed at the beginning that no matter what happened, we'd stick together and finish this great work."

Now they were well into the second month of repairing the dam, and the work was going nicely. When the beavers of Beavercity had taken their turn at building, other beavers from village mounds around the city came forward to take their place.

Every day volunteers reported for work. There was good cooperation, and the leaders had things organized well. This was teamwork at its best.

So the rebuilding of the dam continued.

When Tallabnas saw that he could do nothing to stop them from repairing the dam, he got the jitters. He knew that once the dam was completed, the residents of Beavercity would be protected and strong.

That would make it all the more difficult for Tallabnas to raid them. But if he didn't rob them, where would he get all the food and other supplies he needed to support himself and his gang?

"We have to do something to stop them from completing the dam," Tallabnas growled, slapping his tail down so hard it stung. "But what? This has gone far enough. I'm getting nervous about the whole thing."

"We'll be in deep trouble if we can't raid Beavercity and go plundering in Beaverlake," agreed Mesheg, his counselor.

"How are we going to stop those stubborn beavers from rebuilding their dam?" Tallabnas went on. "Since they came back from being scattered, they seem to be stronger than before the big fight, and firmer on what they set out to do."

"I have an idea," muttered Haibot, another adviser to Tallabnas. "They have huge trust in their leader, Haimehen. They even call him 'Uncle Haim.' We must deal with him. If we can silence Haim, then all the other beavers will swim for their lives."

"That's good thinking," Mesheg chipped in. "So why don't we lure Haim away from the dam, away from his beavers. Let's say we want to talk with him. Suppose we tell him we're ready to make peace with him."

"A great idea!" agreed Tallabnas. "Get him away from the dam and his loyal beavers, and we'll deal with him. Once he's alone, he's ours!" He rubbed his paws together in glee as if he had already taken care of Haim.

One day when Haim and his beavers were up on the dam, doing what they had been doing every day for almost two months, a messenger swam up and greeted him cheerfully.

"I bring you greetings and good news from Tallabnas," he began. "He wants to meet with you. He doesn't want to oppose you any longer. He wants to make peace with you.

"So I have been sent to invite you to meet with Tallabnas in the village of Ono. There you can state your conditions for peace, and my master will slap paws with you. Then you'll be left alone, and there will be peace."

Without even looking down at the messenger, Haim shouted from high up on the dam. "I'm doing a great work! Why should I stop to come and talk with your master?"

That was all. Just that brief reply. But the message was clear, and the messenger had no choice but to take it back to Tallabnas and his advisers.

Four times they sent the messenger back, always with the same message: "Come and talk with us. We want peace."

Four times Haim replied in the same words: "I am doing a great work! Why should I stop to come and talk with your master?"

Haim shouted from the dam, "Why should I stop?"

So the rebuilding of the dam continued.

Not long after that, the messenger came back again. He shouted that his message came directly from the great Tallabnas. His "moles" and spies had brought important information to him, he claimed. This was the message of Tallabnas:

"Your beavers in Beaverlake and Beavercity are getting restless. They are ready to rebel against you. They know what you are planning to do just as soon as you have completed building the dam. You are going to make yourself their number-one leader, Best of the Beavers. They will have no choice but to accept you.

"But they don't want you because you make them work long hours and without pay. Your people are afraid of you. Behind your back they say you are unkind and unfair. So stop now. You're only one against many. You have no chance. I have spoken. I will say no more. Stop now, or you will be ruined. Ruined by your own people!"

When Haim heard that long message, he took a deep breath, snapped the watertight valves on his nose and ears shut, and went down for one of the deepest and longest dives he had ever taken. When he came up at last, he shook the water out of his fur, looked the messenger straight in the eye, and spoke.

"Go back to your master, the mighty Tallabnas, and tell him this: 'You know you are lying! There isn't one bit of truth to your story. You're just trying to scare us into stopping our work.' "

So the rebuilding of the dam continued.

After that, there were no more problems. The

dam was finally finished in early September—exactly fifty-two days after Haimehen and his beavers had begun to rebuild it.

To learn how it really was, read Nehemiah 2:1—6:15. The Haimehen of our story is the Nehemiah of the Bible story, written backward. Tallabnas, the bad guy in our story, is Sanballat in the Bible. The other names—Mallushem, Haibot, and Mesheg—are real Bible names, also written backward (with *sh* counted as one letter).

"What a story!" rattled Robin Raccoon as she sat on the grass chatting with her young friends.

"Kept me guessing all along what was going to happen next," Sammy Squirrel chattered. "That Haimehen story sure had a lot of unexpected turns."

"No matter who you are or where you are, you're going to have problems," stated Tony Turtle.

"That's true," agreed Angora Goat. "But when the Great Spirit is with you, nothing is impossible."

"You're right," yapped Clyde Coyote cheerfully. "But what could the Great Spirit have done without Haim? What a difference one person can make! That sure made me think."

"One person and the Great Spirit," added Robin Raccoon.

The kids were still talking when they heard the

bell for the evening session. They all jumped up and raced for the best seats at the front.

"For tonight's story, we will climb a large hill," began Rabbit, the chairperson, as he raised himself up on his hind legs on the uprooted tree.

"No, no, don't worry! You won't have to leave this lovely spot. Just stay seated on the grass. Our storyteller is going to have us imagine going up a high hill. Are you ready?"

"We're ready!" shouted the crowd. "Let's hear the story!"

"The title is 'Fire in His Belly,'" announced Rabbit. "None other than our good friend Lentulus Leopard is going to tell it. And here is Lentulus."

For a moment the crowd wondered whether Lentulus was going to get on with the story. He spoke in a low voice, seemed embarrassed, and avoided direct eye contact.

Those in front heard him mumble something about being a coward. He said he was ashamed to admit it. But still, he was going to tell it exactly the way it had happened. But he thought it would be best to use his name, Lentulus Leopard, rather than to keep saying *I*.

With that explanation and confession off his tender heart, Lentulus Leopard stood up straight, looked right at his audience, and in a clear voice began his story.

Evening: Leopard's Story

Fire in His Belly

"Oh, please, sir, don't make me go to him," begged Lentulus Leopard. He fell down before Leu the Lion, begging to be excused. "He'll kill me! He'll kill me for sure," he cried, trembling in every part of his body.

Lentulus was terrified. He was sure that if he went to King Baha as a messenger, it would be his death.

"He won't kill you," Leu the Lion assured him, in a calm and even voice. "Just tell him I'm here and I want to see him."

"But you don't understand," stammered Lentulus. "King Baha has been looking for you all over the place. He's sure you are the big mischief-maker. He wants to kill you. Now if I go and tell him you're here, he'll think I belong to you and kill me first. Right on the spot."

"I still think you're mistaken," responded Leu the Lion calmly. "I did ask the Great Spirit not to let it rain for three years. That's why there's nothing growing. That's why everybody is hungry. And that's why King Baha is angry at me. But I had a good reason for doing what I did."

"I know your reason," replied Lentulus. "You have the fire of the Great Spirit burning in your belly. You asked him to punish King Baha and his wicked wife, Lebez, as well as the rest of their Tiger tribe because they stopped believing in the Great Spirit and—"

"Yes, yes, you're absolutely right," Leu the Lion broke in. "They say that there is no Great Spirit; they say that Schlamassel does it all. Well, let me tell you, Lentulus, they're wrong. There is no Schlamassel. He has no eyes, no ears, no mouth, no nothing! He can't see, he can't hear, and he can't talk. He doesn't exist. They made him up."

"I believe that, too. But that's why I'm so afraid to go and tell King Baha that you want to see him. Suppose he asks me if I believe in the Great Spirit, like you do. What will I say?"

"Well, do you?" asked Leu the Lion. "Do you believe in the Great Spirit?"

"Of course I do! With all my heart I believe in the Great Spirit. Schlamassel is nothing!"

"Then you have nothing to fear," stated Leu the Lion. "The Great Spirit will protect you. Go and tell King Baha I want to see him."

Lentulus went as he had been told. He was surprised at his own courage. Suddenly he didn't seem to be afraid about what would happen to him. The important thing was to obey Leu the Lion and get that message to the king of the Tigers.

Leu the Lion was right. Nothing happened to

Lentulus when he delivered the message. But King Baha really pricked up his ears when he heard that Leu the Lion wanted to see him.

"Can you beat that!" he exclaimed. "I've been searching for him all these three years and not found him, and now he comes and says, 'King Baha, I want to see you.' Just like that! Wait till I get my claws on him!"

King Baha thought it best not to tell his wife, Queen Lebez, about the meeting he was planning with Leu the Lion. She was even more furious than her husband about having no rain. She'd shred Leu the Lion into mincemeat before he'd have a chance to pull his tail between his hind legs and run.

The next day King Baha went with the other loyal Tigers to meet Leu the Lion.

"So there you are, you troublemaker!" exclaimed King Baha when he met Leu the Lion. "I've been looking for you in every part of the country."

"I'm not a troublemaker," Leu the Lion declared calmly. "You and your wicked wife, Queen Lebez, are the cause of all this trouble. You rejected the Great Spirit and urged the rest of your Tigers to reject him, too. That's why there's been no rain."

"Why, you mean mongrel! You scum of all the lowdown animals! How dare you talk to me like that!" snarled Baha, king of the Tigers. "Don't you know that one word from me and my Tigers will chomp you in pieces!"

"Still braying like a jackass, are you?" scoffed

Leu the Lion in a voice that showed no fear at all. "Well then, if you're so all-powerful, why don't you make it rain? Go ahead and give the order! Or ask your fake Schlamassel to make it rain."

The two big cats were surely on a collision course. If they had been moose or deer, one could say they were starting to lock horns. It was clear that King Baha had no intention of backing off.

"Okay then," continued Leu the Lion. "Let's fight it out. No, not you and I in a personal fight, and not your people and my people at war. Let your Schlamassel and my Great Spirit fight it out! Let's ask them to show us which one of them is the strongest. How about it? I dare you to a contest!"

King Baha had a score to settle with Leu the Lion, and this seemed to be as good a chance as any to get even with him. He was itching for a good scrap. In such a showdown, his people would see what a great king and leader he really was.

Best of all, he thought, they would see that Schlamassel was as clever and powerful as he and Queen Lebez had always claimed. Why, Schlamassel would knock the stuffing clean out of that so-called Great Spirit invented by Leu the Lion and his people.

So King Baha agreed to have a knockout contest. The queen would love it. His people would love it. It would be better entertainment than a clown, a magician, and a circus all in one. And the victory was absolutely sure.

So they agreed to meet the next day. They didn't have to say "rain or shine," because it had not rained for three years.

The spot they chose for the big event was a hill overlooking all the country of King Baha. The grass that normally would have been lush and green was brown and dead. Way down in the valley below, where the stream normally flowed, Leu the Lion could see the dry gravel and sandy bottom of the riverbed.

The drought was terrible. There was no water even for the birds. Heat waves rolled over the landscape like waves on an imaginary lake. It was all a mirage, like smog drifting over a cemetery. The smell of death was everywhere.

"Listen to me, all you Tigers," roared Leu the Lion. "You know why there has been no rain for three years. You know why the river is dry. You know why this terrible thing has happened to you."

Baha was about to interrupt and say that everybody knew it was because he, Leu the Lion, was the troublemaker. But he changed his mind and kept quiet. Leu the Lion continued.

"Here is your troublemaker," he declared, pointing to King Baha. "He and his wicked wife, Queen Lebez, have led you astray. They told you that there is no Great Spirit. Instead of believing the Great Spirit and following him, you accepted that scarecrow Schlamassel.

"That's right, he is a scarecrow and nothing more. You know what the difference is between a real person and a scarecrow? The scarecrow is just dressed up to look like a real person, but he's stuffed with straw. Did you hear me? His belly and his head are nothing but straw! He has no eyes, no ears, no mouth."

Leu the Lion had expected booing and catcalls, but now he was surprised that everybody kept quiet. Nobody moved, and nobody said a word. King Baha, too, kept his peace—at least for the time being. So Leu the Lion went on.

"Now why do you keep quiet? If you're so sure that your Schlamassel is not a scarecrow, a mere dummy, why don't you shout back your answer? I'll tell you why you're quiet. You aren't sure. Partly you believe and partly you don't believe. You're on the fence."

Leu the Lion had more to say, but he knew that this was not easy for his audience to hear. He wanted to make sure that they understood him. So he paused a moment and looked around. Nobody moved and nobody said anything.

"Your King Baha and I have agreed that today we're going to have this thing settled once and for all. We're going to ask both Schlamassel and the Great Spirit to show their strength. Whoever is stronger, that is the one to follow."

Leu the Lion waited for everyone to cheer, but they were still silent. Yet he could tell that they were deeply interested in the outcome of this contest.

"One more thing before we start," added Leu the Lion. "King Baha's team will go first. Take all the time you need. Do whatever seems right to you.

"Here's the big rock that has to be split. You ask Schlamassel to knock it to pieces, and after that I'll ask the Great Spirit to shatter it. Whoever can do it is the winner. That's fair enough. Have fun!"

Immediately the crowd came alive. First they rushed closer to the rock to examine it. It was huge, big enough for ten animals to sit on. There wasn't a crack in it. It seemed to be solid granite, and had probably been there for thousands of years. The weather had worn the surface smooth.

While they got ready to have their Schlamassel smash that rock, Leu the Lion went off to the side to talk quietly with the Great Spirit. He didn't actually say the words, but the Great Spirit understood that his honor was at stake. This was not an arm-wrestling contest. This was for real!

When Leu the Lion came back to the rock, he found all the Tigers dancing around it and yelling at the top of their voices. Some shouted one thing, and others shouted another.

What Leu the Lion heard more often than anything else was the word "Schlamassel." They called his name over and over again. They pleaded with him, and they urged him to smash that rock. They begged him and they commanded him. But the rock just sat there. Three hours later, there still wasn't a crack in it.

"Shout louder!" mocked Leu the Lion. "Maybe your dummy Schlamassel has ears after all."

And they did shout louder. Leu the Lion laughed. "Perhaps Schlamassel is taking a nap. Wake him up. Perhaps he's in the bathroom. Get him out!"

By now it was midafternoon and the Tigers

were in a frenzy. They were leaping and dancing, running and jumping, shouting and screaming, but the rock was there just as before. It didn't tremble or shake, not even a wee bit. There was no crack in it.

Leu the Lion raised his voice above the din of the crowd and roared again, "Louder, louder! Perhaps Schlamassel is on a journey. He's far away and can't hear you."

The Tigers did shout louder. They ranted and raved until they were all hoarse. They dashed themselves against the big rock until their bones cracked and they were bloody. But nothing happened.

"Schlamassel, hear us!" they wailed. "Schlamassel, don't let us down! Schlamassel, crack that rock! Schlamassel, do it now!"

Totally tired, they finally gave up. Most of them just fell to the ground and lay there panting. All their strength had been spent. It had done no good. Schlamassel had not answered their frantic, pitiful calls. He had not cracked the rock.

"Now come closer, all of you," invited Leu the Lion. "You are many, and I am alone. You made a lot of noise, and I will just speak in a normal voice. You took a long time, and I will be brief. You were worried, and I am sure!"

Then taking a step away from the great rock, he raised his front paws into the sky. "Great Spirit, you have heard these blinded and foolish creatures calling to their scarecrow Schlamassel to crack this rock. He didn't do it because he's just a dummy. But you are real. Show your power now, so they will believe you and follow you."

Leu the Lion was about to say something else, but he didn't because at that moment there was such an ear-splitting crack that it almost threw the Tigers to the ground. To their amazement, they saw that the big rock had been split from top to bottom into two parts!

While they stood there with their mouths wide open, smaller cracks kept showing as the rock continued to split and crumble. While they watched in wonder, it became nothing but a heap of stones, none bigger than a fist.

There was a brief silence. Suddenly the crowd burst out shouting, "The Great Spirit is alive! The Great Spirit did it! We follow the Great Spirit!"

When Leu the Lion looked around, he could not see Baha, King of the Tigers, anywhere.

But he did see a small cloud in the sky. The Tigers were hugging each other and shaking the paws of Leu the Lion. Just then one of them shouted in a voice filled with surprise and joy, "I felt a raindrop!"

"Home, all of you!" commanded Leu the Lion, cheerfully. "Run, before the rain overtakes you."

He spoke too late. Large clouds drifted overhead, and soon the rain was pouring down in torrents. The river in the valley below was filling up again, and the land was coming alive. Trees and grass, animals and birds, and all nature drank their fill of the precious liquid.

Although it rained for a long time, all that water could not put out the fire that was burning in the belly of Leu the Lion.

You may want to check this story against the original report in 1 Kings 18.

After the meeting, some of the youngsters sat around in a cluster discussing what they had just heard.

"No wonder King Baha ducked out after that rock fell apart," said one of them. "He ran to save his hide."

"That story showed me how fickle we sometimes are," added another. "If those Tigers had been smart, they would have known that there just had to be a Great Spirit. How come they fell for that fairy-tale Schlamassel?"

"Folks want to believe something," explained a third. "Everybody does. But they don't think for themselves. The one with the loudest voice and the smoothest tongue can wrap them around their paw like a vine."

"It happens all the time. Why last week—"

Just then Beaver came walking by, and all the kids turned to him to tell him how much they had enjoyed his story that afternoon.

"Tonight's story was rather short," noted Fanny Fox. "There's lots of time left this evening. Would you please tell us another story?"

"Yes, please tell us a bedtime story," they all begged. "Just a short little story, just for us kids. Please, Brother Beaver, please."

Beaver agreed. He sat down with them and scratched his head. "Oh my! The things I get myself into. Here I am thinking of telling you one of the biggest and longest stories I know, and I want to do it in just a few minutes. But let me try.

"This is one of the oldest stories told in our family. It goes right back to the beginning of things. When my grandfather told it, he called it 'The Raft.' Let me see if I remember it.

"Oh, by the way, the Beaver mentioned in that story was one of my earliest relatives long, long ago. So the story is true.

"If you're ready, just sit back and listen. I'll just call it what my grandfather called it, and what his grandfather before him called it: The Raft."

Bedtime: Beaver's Story 2

The Raft

Every day more animals came by to see Beaver build his raft. He didn't mind showing it to them and answering their questions, but he became worried about time. He had a deadline for finishing the raft. But his three sons were good carpenters, too, and together they'd manage.

"Why are you building this raft?" asked a big brown bear.

"We'll need it," replied Beaver, and he kept working and supervising his sons.

"Why are you making it so big?" a moose wondered.

"So there'll be room for lots of animals," Beaver responded.

A friend dropped by. "Who told you to build this raft?"

Beaver took him aside and whispered something into his ear. His friend gave him a long and strange look. He walked away shaking his head.

After that, many more animals came to see the unusual raft. Some began to make fun of it. Then more did. Just to say "raft" became a joke and an occasion for laughter.

"Why don't you build it in the water?" chattered a chipmunk. "Will your raft float on dry land?" He laughed and ran away.

"We heard that your Great Spirit asked you to build that thing," mocked a lion. "Now if that doesn't beat everything! Beaver's been listening to ghosts!"

All this made Beaver's sons upset and discouraged. They wanted to build only at night when the other animals were asleep. But Father Beaver said they shouldn't pay much attention to them. After all, that's what one might expect from beasts who didn't believe in the Great Spirit.

One day, however, it was almost too much for Father Beaver, too. A small delegation of animals came to talk with him. They asked the usual questions and got the usual answers. Then the leader, a huge and serious-looking tiger, spoke for them all.

"Mr. Beaver, you've been in our community a long time. We respect you and your wife, your sons and their wives. But this nonsense with the raft has gone too far.

"At first we thought you were just making a river raft, or teaching your sons a new skill. But now, just look at it! It's enormous! Why, it's big enough for hundreds of animals. Everybody is talking about it—and about you."

He hesitated a moment and then went on. "I don't know how to say this, but others are suggesting. . . ." He hesitated again, and then continued, "They say you're out of your mind."

"I know." Beaver was not at all surprised or upset. "They've told me that to my face."

"How old are you, if I may ask?" asked Tiger.

"Next month I'll be 600," replied Beaver with a smile. "The Great Spirit has been good to me." He excused himself and said he had work to do, a schedule to meet.

Tiger and the others walked away shaking their heads. "Crazy!" Tiger declared.

"Out of his mind," another agreed.

"He's so old his brain has gone soft," remarked a third animal.

"Whose brain wouldn't when you've lived that long!" someone scoffed. "Of course he's not 600 years old. Nobody lives that long. The poor fellow doesn't even know how old he is. But why isn't he dead yet?"

"To think we had to listen to that garbage about all of us dying soon in a big flood," muttered Moose. "He says he knows! Ha, ha! Claims the Great Spirit told him so!" They all laughed heartily.

After a while, the animals stopped talkig about Beaver and his wild project, the raft. It wasn't news anymore.

Then one day there was a heavy rainstorm. Everybody crawled into their shelters for protection. The rain continued all night and all the next day. Soon their homes and burrows were flooded.

The animals scrambled for higher ground. All the lowland was under water. It rained all week. Animals were drowning, and so were the birds, who could find no place to perch and rest. Dead bodies were floating everywhere.

Tiger had also been forced out of his hut by the water. He climbed the nearest hill. When the water reached the top of the hill, he climbed an oak tree.

He sat up there all day, but the water reached the top of the tree. There was only one thing left for him to do: swim. Just swim. Swim without knowing where to swim to. There was no land in sight anymore.

Tiger was struggling to survive, but he could swim no more. His strength was gone. He was exhausted.

Just then he spotted a huge raft floating peacefully in the distance. There were animals of every kind on it.

"BEAVER!" he called. "BEAVER, SAVE ME! I didn't . . . [gulp] . . . mean it!"

He called again and again. But it was too late. The raft was too far away. He sank and never came up again.

In the Bible, this story is in Genesis 6:12-22 and 7:1-24.

Second Day

The second day of the Storytime Jamboree was as beautiful as the first. A clear blue sky, warm sunshine, a gentle breeze, and lots of green grass to sit on. During free time, the younger generation splashed about in the river while their parents strolled in the shaded forest.

"I heard that Beaver told the kids another story last night after we thought it was all over," simpered Simon Skunk.

"Yes, my boy told me," chattered Charlie Chipmunk. "He's a good storyteller. What's the story about this morning?"

"I heard it was something about an uneven fight," Simon Skunk said. "Something about a weasel fighting a bear. But that can't be possible. Probably got it wrong."

"Look, everybody is following Rabbit to the fallen tree," noted Charlie Chipmunk. "That means storytime is about to begin. Let's hurry so we won't miss anything."

Chairman Rabbit was up on his perch, smiling from one floppy ear to the other. "Come closer, everybody!" he called. "What a wonderful day! Isn't it just glorious! And we have another great storyteller this morning. It is none other than Walter Wolf himself.

"His story is about a fight, and his great-grandfather actually saw it. I'll let Walter tell it the way it has been passed on in his family for generations."

Morning: Wolf's Story

The Big Fight

Nobody could remember just how it had started. The parents repeated what they had heard from their grandparents, and the grandparents passed on the stories they heard from their parents. The Grizzlies were a bad bunch!

Every Weasel in the valley and every Weasel on the hills knew it. Don't get close to a Grizzly bear. Avoid all contact with Grizzlies. Never, never tangle with a Grizzly.

"Why are the Grizzlies mad at us?" asked Willy Weasel. His mother looked at him as if he should know the answer.

Surely Willy understood why the Grizzlies and the Weasels were enemies. But the longer his mother thought about it, the less sure she was herself. Yes, why were they enemies?

At last she answered Willy, "I think it's because a long time ago we took away some of their land. At least that's what the Grizzlies say."

"Is it true? Did we take land from them?"

"No we didn't, not really. Well, maybe somewhat. Actually, we just moved in beside them. We lived mostly in the hills, and they lived on the plains and down by the sea.

"There was lots of land, enough for them and us. But over the years, we multiplied and needed more land. So bit by bit, as we claimed more land. The Grizzlies moved away because there wasn't room for all of us."

"Why did we move in with the Grizzlies in the first place?" asked Willy.

"After we came up from the South, we had to go somewhere. But you're too young to understand all this. The Great Spirit told us to settle here."

Whenever Mother Weasel mentioned the Great Spirit, which was not often, she paused before saying the words, as if they were special. Willy noticed this and wondered what it was about the Great Spirit that was so unusual. All the adult Weasels seemed to know.

Once he actually heard his father talking to the Great Spirit. But Willy couldn't see him.

Willy asked no more questions. He had other things to do, especially on this day. He had an important errand to run for his family.

"Here is the lunch." His mother handed him a bag. "Be sure to find your brothers and give it to them. Don't give it to anyone else."

Willy promised and ran off. He was happy to take the lunch to his two brothers. This would give him a chance to watch the big fight.

His brothers and all the other grown-up Weasels had gone off to fight the Grizzlies more than a week ago. Willy wanted so much to see the fight, but his parents wouldn't let him go. They said he was too young.

So this was his happy day. He had to carry the lunch to his brothers, and nobody could stop him.

When he came to the top of the hill where the Weasel tough guys were gathered, he could tell right away that they were in a bad mood. They weren't fighting at all. They were standing around in small groups, talking in low whispers, sometimes just standing there as if frightened.

Always they were looking across the valley to the hill on the opposite side. That hill was covered with Grizzlies like trees in a forest. As far as Willy could see, there were Grizzlies.

As he searched for his brothers among the Weasels, he heard one declare, "It's no use! We can't beat him."

He moved on and heard another say, "If you ask me, I think we should forget the whole thing and go home." They certainly were a discouraged bunch. There was no fight in them.

As Willy picked his way through the Weasel camp, he wondered what that Weasel had meant by saying "We can't beat him." Who was he talking about?

Willy pushed on to find his brothers and give them their lunch. Few Weasels paid any attention to him. Once or twice somebody asked what a kid like him was doing out here at the battle.

He told them that he had brought lunch for his brothers. Then he asked if they knew where he could find them. Nobody seemed to know. There were so many Weasels.

At last he saw them, way over on the far side of the hill. He ran as fast as he could, holding up his lunch bag for them to see. If he had expected a warm welcome, he was mistaken.

To his surprise, his oldest brother asked in a rough voice, "Willy, what in the world are you doing here? Now you go right back where you came from. You hear me!"

"I brought your lunch. Mother asked me to bring it to you."

As he handed the bag to them, he noticed the same fear on their faces that he had seen on the others. They didn't seem hungry. He wanted to ask why they were scared and why they weren't fighting the Grizzlies, but he didn't dare.

Instead of thanking him for bringing the lunch, his older brother griped, "We know why you came here. You just wanted to see the fight, that's why! Well, the fight hasn't started yet. Perhaps there won't be any fight. You're too young to watch, anyway.

"So why don't you just beat it? Go on home and stay there! This is no place for kids!"

Just then there was a commotion among the Weasels as they all turned to face the valley below. Everybody wanted to get the best view. The Grizzlies were lining up on the hill on the opposite side of the valley. They had been there for days.

Before long, they heard a loud voice that made everyone tremble. "Come and fight me!" roared the voice. "If you beat me, the land is yours. If I beat you, the land is ours!"

Willy didn't know that this drama had been acted out every day for almost a week. Usually in the middle of the morning or in early afternoon, the largest of the Grizzlies, a huge monster, would strut down the hill right to the gully that divided the valley.

He'd stand there a while, flexing his muscles and showing off his size. Then he'd walk around and stomp his big feet, making the earth shake. He'd make a few scary noises but not say anything.

He had the full attention of all the Weasels and knew they were so scared that their blood was running cold. Each day he'd bellow the same words to them, "Come and fight me!"

When nobody came, he'd keep up the roaring. "Why, you yellow-livered Weasels, what's the matter with you? You aren't scared of me, are you? Just send one of your brave Weasels down to fight with me, and we'll soon know whose land this is!"

On the Grizzly Hill, they waited for an answer. It never came. They waited for a Weasel to come down into the valley and challenge their chosen hero, the Great Grizzly, but nobody came. The humongous fellow stood there ready to fight, but he had no contestant.

After roaring a few more challenges and insults at the Weasels, the giant gave all his comrades on the hill a signal. Instantly the entire valley, from one end to the other, was filled with shouting and roaring, frightening noises.

All the Weasels' hearts dried up in their chests. They had no strength or courage left to go out and fight the Grizzlies. Not after seeing the Great Grizzly and hearing all the others.

Willy understood why the Weasels were standing around in small clusters whispering. He understood why some thought they should just forget the whole thing and go home. To match one Weasel against that big hulk called the Great Grizzly would be like sending a fly to fight an elephant.

Then Willy had an idea. He asked to be taken to the commander of the Weasels.

As soon as Willy Weasel was introduced to the commander, he announced, "I will go down and fight that monster."

"That's noble of you, my lad," replied the commander. "But you would be going straight to your death.

"Have you seen how strong the Great Grizzly is? Have you seen how tall he is when he stands on his hind legs? With his big front paws, he could wipe you out with one swipe. Just one swat, and you would be mush!"

"That may be true," Willy responded, "but you overlook one important detail. The Great Spirit is on our side. If I ask the Great Spirit to help me, I can kill that monster."

Willy was surprised to hear himself mention the Great Spirit. It was the first time he had ever done that. But having said it, he believed it. Like his mother, he believed that with the Great Spirit on his side, he could do what needed to be done.

The commander was silent a long time. He was thinking. Then he exclaimed, "But you are just a youth! You have no experience in fighting. Just look at the Great Grizzly. He's an old fighter. He knows all the tricks. I'd hate to send your limp body home to your parents."

"There is no need to worry about that," Willy assured him. "With all due respect, Commander, the problem with you and all the other Weasels is that you keep looking at the Great Grizzly until you can see nothing else.

"I see him too, but I believe that the Great Spirit will help me. I am not afraid. Please let me go down and fight this giant."

The commander was impressed. He thought for a moment and then declared in a loud voice for all the Weasels to hear, "We have a volunteer to go down to meet the Great Grizzly!"

Turning to Willy, he muttered, almost in a whisper, "I wish you well. This is going to be a day that will long be remembered in our history."

Then he called several Weasel officers and told them to give Willy a few quick lessons in fighting.

"Now this is how you do it," began one of the officers. "You stand right in front of the Grizzly and try to send a spear through his heart. Here, take this spear and practice a bit."

Willy took the spear, but it was too heavy. He could hardly lift it. If he had to drag that thing around, he would be in trouble. He gave it back to the captain.

"All right, so that doesn't work," agreed another officer. "Then why don't you try this?" He gave a few fancy strokes with his sword, but Willy wasn't sure that he understood any of it. By now, he wasn't sure he needed any of their advice.

When Willy's brothers heard that he had offered to take care of the Great Grizzly, they were furious. They tried to stop him, but it was too late. Not only had Willy made up his mind to go and fight the big brute, but the commander had given him permission.

The brothers walked back to their places, grumbling and wondering what they would say to their mother when the Great Grizzly killed their kid brother.

Meanwhile, Willy seemed to be feeling bolder with every step he took down the hill. He walked in light steps, as though he were just out for a stroll. Long before he had reached the valley below, he felt sure he could knock out the Grizzly. He didn't quite know how, but he was confident.

At last Willy arrived where the big Grizzly stood waiting for him. Then suddenly his mood changed, and he wasn't sure at all that he should have volunteered for this. The Great Grizzly had looked big from the distance, but from close up, he seemed enormous.

Willy noticed his paws. If one of them landed on top of him, there would be nothing left but crushed bones and a mass of mincemeat. He gaped at the Great Grizzly's head, way up in the sky, almost like a treetop. As Willy Weasel looked up at him, those eyes looked like coals of fire set in two sockets of a brown, woolly, and moving monster.

Suddenly the Great Grizzly opened his mouth and let out a bellow that almost turned Willy's bones to jelly. He felt weak in his knees. This was a lot more frightening than he had expected.

"Have you come out to make fun of me?" snorted the big one. Then he turned to the Weasels on the hill and roared, "Don't you have a soldier to come and fight with me? Why do you send this kid?"

The Weasels did not respond. Willy didn't say anything either. He was studying the movements of his challenger. His heart was beating wildly. The terror had left him; he wasn't really afraid anymore, but he was worried. He knew that any moment might be his last. And the fight had not yet begun.

"Well, little one," growled the Great, looking down from his lofty height. "What are we going to do about this? Shall I kill you with one blow, or shall we warm up first and then make it at least look like we're fighting?"

Willy still stood right in front of the Grizzly. Since the bear had raised himself up on his hind legs, Willy did the same. If it hadn't been such a serious moment, it would have been quite funny. The Great Grizzly was about ten feet tall and Willy not much more than ten inches tall. No wonder the Grizzly was disgusted.

"Why don't I just step on you?" growled the big one. "You'll never know what hit you."

"Go ahead," yelled Willy, "just try it!"

So the Great Grizzly did. But Willy was too fast. He jumped out of the way. That made the Grizzly angry.

"There's just one thing you should know before

we start fighting for real," cried Willy. "You are big and I am little. You are strong and I am weak. You are an experienced soldier and I am only a youth.

"But what you don't know is that I've got something you don't have. I have the Great Spirit on my side. Before the sun sets tonight, you'll be dead!"

The Great Grizzly let out such a big laugh that all the Grizzlies and all the Weasels heard it on their hills. Then he turned and with one swift swat of his right paw, he came down on Willy.

Except that Willy wasn't there! He had expected that paw and like a flash had jumped to the side.

Now the struggle was beginning in earnest. The Great Grizzly lurched forward to step on Willy again, but missed him the second time. He waved his huge paws about him like a windmill, but every time he thought he had Willy, he had missed him.

Whenever the Great Grizzly tried to clap Willy between his front paws and crush him, or grab him and dash him to the ground, Willy got away.

Meanwhile, Willy was finding his own strategy. He dashed this way and that, jumped into the air, and danced about like the slick animal he was. The Great Grizzly tried to keep an eye on him, which meant that he had to keep turning all the time.

One moment Willy was in front of him, and the next moment he was behind him. The Great Grizzly didn't like it when he couldn't see Willy, even if it was only for a few seconds. It made him nervous. He was especially uneasy when Willy was behind him. By the time he had turned his big body around, Willy had already dashed off to another spot.

Sometimes the Great Grizzly would lurch forward, thinking that this time he could step on Willy. But he always missed him. When Willy was in just the right spot for a quick kill, the Great Grizzly would stretch out his huge paw and swat away. But he always missed. Willy was too fast for him.

As Willy dashed about, he felt strange. He was like a spinning top, spun by an outside power. He felt as if someone was lifting him up and hurling him on, almost as if a great wind was carrying him along. But there was no wind, and Willy knew that he was not alone. The Great Spirit was there with him.

Again the Great Grizzly thought the moment for a strike had come, but again he missed. Willy wasn't running anymore. He was leaping in circles around the Bear.

Willy swished through the air in one moment and slithered low in the grass the next moment. Now he looked like a bird flying, and then he looked like a snake slithering. The Great Grizzly was bewildered and getting confused. He couldn't keep up with him.

As the Great Grizzly kept turning and twisting in response to Willy's rapid movements, he was getting dizzy. Willy knew what he was doing. Faster and faster he flew around the Bear. Now he went clockwise, then suddenly he changed and went counterclockwise.

Willy and the Great Grizzly

Clearly Willy was on the offensive and the Grizzly on the defensive. The Grizzly stopped swatting and stomping his feet in an effort to strike Willy. He had all he could do to keep an eye on him. The Great Grizzly suspected that Willy wanted to jump on him from behind or do something else to him in an unguarded moment.

On both hills there was silence. In amazement the Grizzlies watched how their hero was being worn out and confused by that whippersnapper of a weasel.

On the opposite hill, the Weasels were watching with open mouths. They saw how their own little Willy was playing with the Grizzly as if he were a toy. But they all knew that this was no game. This was a matter of life and death.

Once the Great Grizzly thought he had figured out Willy's movements and expected him to reverse his rapid racing around him. But to his surprise, Willy kept going in the same direction. Faster and faster he flew, now down in the grass and then up in the air. Now leaping and then slithering.

For a brief moment, the Bear thought he might just stand still and let Willy whirl around him. But when he tried it, he realized that when Willy was behind him, he was not protected. So he kept rotating like a merry-go-round, trying to face the leaps and slithers of Willy.

Faster and faster he turned as Willy increased his tempo. The Bear's head was spinning, and he was so dizzy that he was staggering and could hardly stay upright.

That was the moment Willy had been waiting for. As if stopped by a wall, Willy suddenly stood stock still. The Bear tried to stop too, but couldn't. He had been spinning so long and so fast, and he had too much momentum to stop that abruptly.

In addition, he was dizzy. Terribly dizzy. Sick and dizzy. He slowed down. He stumbled. He fell with a thud that echoed in the hills.

The hero of the Grizzlies, the Great Grizzly himself, lay flat on the ground. He was groaning and breathing hard.

Almost faster than their eyes could follow, the Grizzlies and the Weasels on both hills saw Willy leap at the throat of the fallen giant. He knew where to go for the big artery, and his teeth were sharp. Willy bit once, and blood appeared. He bit a second time, but the damage was already done.

The Great Grizzly struggled to get up but lost his balance and fell down again. He tried several more times, and at last he did manage to get to his feet. But all he could do was stumble around, let out some horrible growls, and fall down again.

He was bleeding fast. The grass all around him was turning red. He wanted to get up but couldn't. He lifted his big right paw to swat at Willy, but it was nothing but a weak and aimless motion.

Then he quit trying, but his big hulk of a body was still shaking. The strong muscles in his shoulders were still twitching. Finally the shaking and twitching stopped. He lay there like an oversized, stuffed sack, silent and without motion.

The Great Grizzly was dead!

When the commander of the Weasels saw what had happened, he shouted just one order: "After them!"

All the Weasels raced down the valley and up the other side of the hill to give chase to the Grizzlies. The bears were running in great confusion in all directions, just as fast as they could go.

After that, the Grizzlies left the Weasels alone. Willy Weasel became a household name. Everybody talked about him and how he had beaten the Bear and saved the Weasel nation.

If you would like to compare the above with the original story, take your Bible and read 1 Samuel 17.

"An incredible story!" exclaimed Rony Raccoon. "If Wolf hadn't told it, I would have trouble believing it. But Wolf tells the truth."

"Exactly. And the storytellers have strict orders to tell only true stories," added Margaret Muskrat. "I am impressed that young Willy Weasel was so sure the Great Spirit would help him."

"Remember," Rony Raccoon rattled, "Willy grew up with parents who believed in the Great Spirit. His mother would say that name with special awe, and his father was actually talking to him. The kid believed because his parents believed."

"You're probably right," agreed Margaret Muskrat. "But after this experience with the

Great Grizzly, he'll believe not just because his parents did, but because of his own experience. By the way, I heard that Beaver is to tell us another story this afternoon. I sure don't want to miss him. He's really good!"

The two friends were still talking when they saw Chairperson Rabbit up on his perch, waving his arms for people to come closer. It was time for the meeting to begin.

"Welcome back, everybody," said Rabbit. "This afternoon we are going to hear a story about—" Rabbit stopped abruptly. Then he continued, "Why should I tell you what it's going to be about? We have the storyteller himself up here to tell us that. Give a big paw to our friend Beaver."

Beaver got up, and when the cheering noise and commotion had died down, he began. "Every story must have a title, even if it's just one word, but I don't know what to call this one.

"Perhaps 'One Beaver Did, And One Beaver Didn't.' But that doesn't really say it. Then I thought I'd call it 'The Beaver That Left and Came Back.' But that's no good either because it says too much.

"The title of a story shouldn't give away the story. It should only hint at it. A good title should be a puzzle and keep the listener guessing. So finally I've decided to simply call my story 'The Beaver Brothers.'

"Just one more detail. The story is about two brothers, and my uncle Michael was that younger brother in this story. This is how he told it to me."

Afternoon: Beaver's Story 3

The Beaver Brothers

"There's no end to this work," complained Michael to his older brother, Sam. "We work, work, work! And what do we get for it? Nothing!"

"That's not true," replied Sam. "You well know what we get. When our parents—"

"Ya, ya, I know. When our parents die, everything they have will belong to us. You know what I call that? Pie in the sky by and by."

"That's right," Sam went on. "When our parents die, we get the pie, as you call it. And I remind you that it's no small pie."

"But until then, we have nothing but work and more work," complained Michael.

"We beavers have a good life because we work," stated Sam, with special emphasis on the word *because*. "Ever hear them say 'busy as a beaver'? That's us! It's our nature to work and to be busy."

"But work is more than just keeping us busy. Work builds our shelters, work produces food for our bodies, work constructs dams, and work—"

"Ya, ya, ya!" interrupted the younger brother,

not convinced. "And now you're going to tell me that on top of everything else, work is good for us."

Then, imitating Sam and what Sam had told him a hundred times, Michael sang out through his nose, "Work builds character."

"You said it!" responded Sam, the older brother, as he pulled another log out of the water and struggled to put it into place. "Here, why don't you help me with this? Soon we'll have another dam finished."

"There's another word that rhymes with dam," grumbled Michael, "but I'm not allowed to say it. Right now, I sure would like to."

"Mind your tongue," snapped Sam as if he were a schoolteacher. "The only thing you prove when you use bad language is that you don't know many words."

"Ya, ya, and you've told me that before, too," griped Michael. "Okay then, I won't say the word.

"But you know what word really tells the story of our life? It's the word *another*. There's always *another* dam to build and *another* dam to repair, *another* tree to cut down and *another* log to put in place.

"I don't think that's what I want to do the rest of my life. There's more to living than work. I want to enjoy myself!"

"You're too young to know what you want," declared Sam, the older brother. "Beavers are born for work. We thrive on work. Ever see a beaver get into mischief? Of course not! And I'll tell you why not—"

"Never mind! I know that," groaned Michael

wearily. "If you've told me once, you've told me a dozen times: 'Idleness is the devil's workshop.' And because we beavers are never idle, we never give the devil a chance to get us into trouble."

Michael was not in a good mood. They were floating that log along the edge of the bank, trying to push it closer to the half-finished dam, when he picked up the conversation again.

"The reason you never get into trouble, Sam, is because you keep all the rules. I don't how you do it. How can you even remember them all? 'Don't do this,' and 'don't do that.' No wonder they call you a 'goody.' "

"Now you cut that out and get to work," snapped Sam just as Father Beaver came swimming up to them with some twigs in his mouth.

"We'll stick these twigs in the cracks between the logs and plaster them in place with mud," he explained.

He began pushing them into the cracks when he noticed Michael sitting there pouting. He wondered why he looked so unhappy.

"Any problems this morning?" he asked kindly, not addressing the question to anyone in particular.

"Go ahead, tell him what you just told me," urged Sam. Then he climbed out of the water and turned to his father. "I think Michael has something he wants to say to you."

Michael was not ready to be put on the spot so suddenly. It is one thing to speak your mind to your older brother. But it's quite another thing to repeat it to your father. He hesitated.

These thoughts were not yet ripe, and he hadn't discussed them with anyone else. Slowly he shook the water out of his fur, sat down on a log, and after a few uncertain starts, he spoke to his dad.

"Sam and I were just talking about the purpose of life and whether work is the only thing we're here for. As you know, he never stops working, except to eat and sleep. He thinks work is our greatest blessing.

"I thought perhaps I could have some fun, especially since I'm still young."

He stopped. First he looked at his brother as if to say, Look what you got me into. Then he turned toward his father, and his face said, Do you know what I'm talking about?

Father Beaver knew exactly what he was talking about. "Let's all sit here for a bit and discuss it," he suggested, moving onto the green grass of the bank.

Sam wasn't sure it needed to be discussed. Everything was as clear as the water in the lake. There was work to be done. But when he saw his father's look, he came out of the water and joined them on the bank.

Yes, Sam was an obedient son. Like now, the father didn't even have to speak. Just a look, and he obeyed him.

"You're both right," began Father Beaver kindly. "Work is wonderful, but life is more than work. There is a place for fun. Clean wholesome fun.

"First let's look at work. We need to work if we are to have shelters and food. Just look out over this pond and see all those domes. Each one is a home for ten or more beavers. Isn't it a magnificent sight!"

As they looked, they could see dozens of dome-shaped lodges sticking out of the water like so many little islands. The biggest part of them was under water, Michael knew.

With the sun shining and the birds singing, the sight of this beaver community was enough to fill any heart with pride. Beavers were swimming about, attending to their business, while the little ones were splashing each other.

"Now you know that all those houses had to be build out of logs and branches, sticks and reeds, and plastered with mud," continued Father Beaver. "They had to be made solid below and weatherproof above the surface.

"In winter, when the water freezes, our houses above the water become as hard as the ice around them. Yet inside they are dry and cozy. To make sure that we are also safe, we have our tunnels and doors under the water."

"And all that just happens by itself?" interrupted Sam with a smirk on his whiskered face. He thought he was helping his father make the point.

"Of course not," replied Michael. "All summer I've helped you build our shelters. We do need them. But it just seems that there is no end to the work."

"One moment, please," said Father Beaver gently. "Let me finish explaining about work before we get to your wish to have some fun too."

They shifted their positions for more comfort, looked around to make sure they were safe, and then Father Beaver continued.

"I won't talk more about the need to build dams, gather and store food, repair our shelters, and everything that goes into making life comfortable. You ask what life is all about and what we're made for. Those are good questions.

"One way to answer is to look at ourselves. I mean, look at the way we're made. Then ask the question, Why are we made that way?"

Both brothers sat up straight, and Father Beaver could tell they hadn't thought about it that way.

"Look at our fur, for example. See how it's made for living in water as well as out of water. Feel the soft and dense underfur next to our skin. That keeps us warm. Now look at our coarse guard hairs that cover the underfur. They're on the outside to keep us dry. They keep the water out. The short soft hairs keep the body heat in, and the long coarse hairs keep the water out."

The brothers examined their double layers of fur as if they had discovered it for the first time. They used a split claw on each hind foot to comb their fur.

Father Beaver continued. "Now look at our teeth. Those yellowish incisors never stop growing. As long as we live, they'll always keep growing. And notice their shape: they're sharp like chisels. That's so we can cut and split wood. Without those teeth, we couldn't build dams or shelters. We wouldn't be beavers."

"I never thought of that," responded Michael. "And of course, without strong teeth and claws, we couldn't move sticks and branches or anything into position to strengthen the dams."

"You're right." Father Beaver was pleased that his sons were listening and learning. It would help them better understand themselves and each other.

"The rest of our body is made for work, too. Our webbed hind feet are for fast swimming, our powerful muscles for moving logs, our noses and ears with watertight valves shutting off for underwater activity— and a lot more.

"Most of all, let me just remind you of one more wonderful gift from the Great Spirit who made us: our precious instinct for community life."

"I knew it, I knew it!" whispered Michael cheerfully. "Father never talks for long without getting onto his favorite subject. Isn't that right?"

Then turning to his father with a smile, Michael added, "We need to hear it! So why don't you go ahead and tell us about our togetherness once more?"

"Okay, so perhaps I do talk about community a lot, but we can never say it too often," declared Father Beaver. "We wouldn't be beavers if our bodies weren't built the way they are. Just as surely, we wouldn't be beavers if we didn't have the urge for sharing life.

"That's why we live in colonies. We want to be together. Long ago beavers may have been loners or perhaps fighters, but not now! That's just not what we are today. We live together because we enjoy each other. We're a peaceful bunch. We think that's the way life should be."

There was a pause, and Father Beaver stroked Michael's glossy brown hair. Then he added, "And that's also why we mate for life. And why we all work together."

He stopped and stretched his long body on the grass during a thoughtful pause. "You know, boys, work is one thing, and working together is another. When we do something together, it's a lot more fun than when we do it alone. And we really do need each other to put some of those big logs in place."

"So you're saying that work is fun?" asked Michael. "But I had in mind *having* fun, not working all the time."

Father Beaver agreed that work and fun could be the same activity and that they could also be separate. Not all work is fun, and one could have fun apart from work.

Just then Sam jumped up and said he had work to do. Before leaving, however, he whispered to Michael, "Why don't you tell him?"

Michael stayed with his father. Perhaps Sam was right. Since he had gone this far in the conversation, he might as well continue. But what he wanted to say was not easy. He tried several times but never managed to say the right words.

Finally he simply asked, "Father, why can't I leave and see something of the world? I know it would hurt you, but after I'm gone a while, you'd get used to being without me."

His father was silent.

"Sam would be with you. He's not interested in the things that I am. He just wants to stay here and work."

Father Beaver wiped a tear from his eye. "If that's what you want, my son, I will not stand in your way. But I'll miss you."

"Thanks a lot." Michael was relieved that the problem was solved. "Now there is one detail that I need to mention, if you don't mind. I don't quite know how to say this, either, but it concerns the things that would be mine one day if I chose to stay home. Could I have some of that now, please?"

"I think we can manage that. You know our custom. When I die, you get one-third, and Sam gets two-thirds because he's the oldest. But since you're planning to leave, I'm willing to stretch the custom and let you have your part now."

"Thanks for understanding, Father. You're really great. I hope Sam won't mind."

"I'll talk with him. He will not be shortchanged. You take your share now, and he'll get his share when I die."

Michael laid his shiny brown paw on the shoulder of his father. "Thanks a lot! You're very kind."

During the next days, there were many preparations for Michael's leaving. His father sold off some lodges to raise the money for his share. Neighbors thought he was crazy to be giving Michael his inheritance in advance.

There were good-byes to his friends and other beavers of the community. It was not easy to leave home and family. However, since he had decided to go, Michael was not going to change his mind now just because leaving was difficult. Early one morning, Michael was off.

He set out to swim directly to the opposite shore of the lake. He had never been there before. He hoped to make it before dark.

Out in the open lake, Michael began to realize that swimming there was quite different from paddling around in his familiar community.

Once a motorboat suddenly appeared out of nowhere, roared right up to him, and would have split his head open if he hadn't made a fast dive.

A little later, when he was tired and climbed on top of a floating log for a rest, he was almost gobbled up by a water snake. That slippery creature sneaked up behind him and gave him such a fright that he didn't stop swimming until he was totally out of breath.

When Michael finally approached the shore, exhausted and hungry, he noticed two men with guns stalking the sandy bank. They seemed ready to shoot anything that moved.

For a moment Michael wondered whether he had made a mistake in leaving home. He knew that his father would be glad to see him back. But when he thought about all that work, sharing his days with his grim brother, Sam, he decided to keep going.

Slowly he realized that there was another reason why he wanted to keep going: adventure. He did want to get away from work and all things so familiar to him at home. In addition, he wanted to have new experiences. Sam couldn't understand him. Michael wondered whether perhaps his father had understood.

He was beginning to understand himself in a way he had never done before. This trip was taking him away from the familiar and moving him into the strange. He was leaving the old and reaching out to the new. That in itself was exciting.

Suddenly he saw it quite clearly: there was both push and pull. The push to leave home, and the pull to explore.

The next day he came to the mouth of a small river. "Might as well see where it leads," he muttered out loud as he left the lake and swam up the river.

It was much harder to swim against the current than he had thought. He had never been in a river before. Progress was slow. But this, too, was a new experience. "Leaving the old, exploring the new," he told himself as he cheerfully pushed on.

After some days, he discovered that the river divided, and he had to decide which fork to take. Since he had no idea where either one would lead to, he decided to take the left fork. It was a good decision. It led him straight into another community of beavers. This is how it happened.

He was swimming along enjoying himself when suddenly he met two young beavers about his own age. They chatted with him for a while, and they told him about their community. They even invited him to go along with them to their settlement.

As they swam along, Michael told them a bit

about his own home. But mostly he talked about his wonderful new life of freedom.

The two young beavers listened eagerly. "Now I'm free," Michael told them. "I never knew what real freedom was until now. No rules! Can you imagine, a life without rules? It's great!"

When he saw the surprised and eager looks on their faces, he continued telling them more about his new life. "And no work! I have a brother back home who works all the time. I have worked a lot, too, but all that is behind me now."

Michael made a fancy curve, slapped the water with his flat tail, and disappeared below. When he came up again, the two young beavers urged him to tell them more about his adventures in freedom. They immediately started to make plans to have all the young beavers gather to meet their new friend.

Soon the trio arrived at that beaver community. It wasn't long until the news of Michael's arrival had reached all the communities along the river.

Beavers came from everywhere to welcome him and chat with him. Every night he stayed up with the young beavers, having a great time. They carried on almost until morning.

Once when Michael thought of getting some sleep at last, he remembered his brother, Sam. He was probably getting up about that time to start work. Poor Sam, thought Michael. In a way he's a good brother. He never does anything wrong. But what does he get out of life? Nothing!

The name "Michael" was on everybody's

tongue. It was "Michael here" and "Michael there." "Michael, when are you throwing another party? . . . Michael, don't forget to invite me to your next feast! . . . Michael, don't forget, I'm your friend."

Michael certainly enjoyed all the attention he was getting. He was popular, especially with the girls. If only once his brother Sam could see how many friends he had! Then Sam would understand what he had meant by saying that life was more than work.

This is what he had wanted when he left home, and he was not disappointed. His cup was full and running over. Parties . . . food . . . girls . . . freedom . . . friends! This was living! Real living!

The summer passed quickly, and the days were getting shorter. Michael gave no thought to winter coming. He hadn't realized that the new life he was living could not continue forever. Certainly he was not prepared for the way it came to an end with a jolt.

Michael was having another fling with his young friends, swimming wild, diving from the top of the dam, dancing late, and living it up. Then they said they were tired of what they were doing and wanted a change. They were hungry and wanted to eat.

Now Michael was in a jam. He had served them his last food. It was all he had. There was nothing left in the bags and boxes, and the bottles were empty.

Everything his father had given him had been spent. It was all used up. His father's savings had been thrown away on wild parties. Michael had nothing left. Nothing!

So he told his young friends that he didn't have anything. He cheerfully suggested that perhaps now it was their turn to pitch in. But they grumbled and called him a spoilsport. Some called him worse names than that. And then they sneaked away.

Michael couldn't believe it. A fine lot of friends they were! As long as he paid for the parties, he was their friend, he was popular. But when he had nothing more to offer, they turned their backs and swam away. They didn't really want *him*, he thought. They only wanted the things he had.

The next day he looked up some of his friends, but they would have nothing to do with him. As far as they were concerned, Michael Beaver was dead. He was alone. He didn't have a friend left.

Still shaking his head bitterly, he slowly paddled out of the community. Following another river, smaller than the first one, he continued eastward until some days later, he happened to catch up with several beavers swimming in the same direction. He was glad to see them and greeted them in a friendly way as he came closer.

"My name is Michael," he introduced himself to a middle-aged beaver. "Mind if I swim along?"

"Not at all," replied the older beaver. "But our journey by water is almost over. Just ahead, we leave this river and start our overland trek."

Michael had never heard of anything like that before. He was curious about why they would travel on land rather in the water.

"We're going home," explained the older beaver. "We left our community a few days ago to explore new settlement possibilities, but we found none. So we're going home to give our report to the others and make plans for the future. You're welcome to come with us."

It sounded strange and mysterious to Michael. Why would a whole colony of beavers want to move and settle somewhere else? He knew why *he* had left home, but he couldn't figure out why so many beavers would want to do that.

Soon the small group left the river and was making its way across the fields. Finally they reached a wooded area, and the oldest beaver, who seemed to be the leader, explained to Michael that they were almost home now. "Our lake is just around the corner."

That's how Michael found himself far away from home in a strange community, surrounded by beavers who had never even heard of his country or his family. These beavers seemed to be having some problem with the weather.

"This is Michael," the older beaver announced to the members of his community that evening after supper. "We met on the way home and invited him to come and eat with us." He told them what little he knew about Michael and suggested that Michael tell them more about himself.

Michael was not used to being so formal. When they all gathered around him, he told about his family back home and that he was just traveling a bit.

He was careful not to mention what he had

done all summer. Certainly he didn't tell them that he had already wasted everything his father had given him.

Michael ended his little speech by asking whether perhaps they had work for him to do. He didn't tell them that he had no food stored up, but he did say that building and dam construction was not new to him.

Several older beavers huddled to discuss his request. Suddenly Michael found it strange to think that he should be *asking* for work. Sam wouldn't believe it if he told him. He remembered the many times at home when he had tried to get out of work. Wouldn't his brother laugh if he knew about this?

For Michael, it was no laughing matter. He needed food, and the only way he could get food was to work for it. He knew that. The only other thing was to starve.

The beavers turned from their huddle and told him they had reached a decision. He could stay. They had a job for him. Not here, but on the other side of the lake. For his work, they would give him a place to sleep and one meal a day.

They apologized for not offering more and explained that they were all having a hard time. There simply wasn't enough food for three meals a day. The lake was drying up, they were worried about their own families, and that was the best they could do. He could take it or leave it.

"I'll take it," he declared, and swam off with two of the older beavers to have a look at the new job. He didn't like it much, but what choice did he have? He didn't want to starve.

In the days and weeks that followed, he almost worked his claws off. He never did get to like what he was doing. It was awful, downright disgusting! Instead of building a shelter or a dam, which he knew how to do, he was told to dig, dig, dig. Instead of swimming around in the cool lake while he worked on a construction project, he had to work on dry land—of all the stupid places! A beaver on dry land! All alone.

Again he was told about the great drought that had come into the country. All the rivers and lakes were drying up. There was this pond, off to one side, not connected to the larger lake where they had their community.

Since the water level in their own lake was sinking every day, there was danger of it drying up altogether. They got the idea that if they could connect that pond to their lake with a canal, then the water from the higher pond would run into their lake and keep it from drying up. His job was to dig that canal.

If he hadn't been so hungry, he would never have taken the job. He remembered his father saying that when the devil is really hungry, he'll eat flies. This was just about as bad as that. Now he was even thankful for this dusty and dirty job, just so he could eat. Even if it was only once a day.

Apart from the hard work and little food, there was another thing that made this job difficult—it was so demeaning, beneath him. After all, he was a beaver, not a badger. He was a builder, not an earthmover. Sure he could do it, but it hurt his pride even more than it hurt his front paws.

Another thing made it hard for him. He had to work alone. It was almost like a punishment, like a prison sentence. There was nobody to talk to all day. That was simply not the way they did things back home.

On one of those days when he could hardly stand the loneliness any longer, he remembered his father's frequent little speeches about "community" and "hanging together." He remembered that, shortly before he left home, he had made light of it when his father had talked about "cooperation" and "togetherness." Now he was sorry he had done that.

It wasn't just the dirty work and doing it alone that upset him. In addition, he never got enough to eat. He was always hungry. Once in a while he'd stop grubbing the earth and sneak away to the pond to find something there. He simply had to have food.

There was usually a plant or two, or a young tree with tender bark that he could quickly strip off and gobble down. Once he found some tender, juicy buds which he deliberately ate slowly to prolong the pleasure. He enjoyed every nibble of it, and with every little swallow, he thought of the good times at home when there had been lots and lots of these buds.

Then the boss beavers found out what he was doing. They told him to cut it out. "You get your one meal a day!" they barked. "Your job is to dig that canal, not to sneak off, stealing food that isn't yours in the first place."

When they talked like that, he boiled inside. He was that mad! But he didn't show it on the outside. He didn't want to get into more trouble than he already had. He dare not lose his job.

Days stretched into weeks and weeks into months. If his partying friends from the other community had met Michael now, they would hardly have recognized him. He had lost a lot of weight, and his once-shiny brown fur was a dull and dusty gray. Several front teeth were broken, and his paws looked a mess. They were swollen, raw, and wounded from ripping at the earth.

Most shocking was the changed expression on Michael's face. There was no smile and no laughter. Some days he spoke no more than ten words. There was no one to talk to.

He was always alone and so exhausted that when he stopped working in the evening, he ate his one meal and promptly dropped off to sleep. His eyes had lost their lively twinkle, his voice was husky, and there were times when his mind just went blank.

One day during the sixth month away from home, he was having a really hard time with the canal. In his digging and earthmoving, he ran into stones and rocks that had to be moved. How he wished for at least one other beaver to help him with the big ones, but there was nobody!

It was a hot day, and he was thirsty. As usual, he was also hungry. Just when he wanted to risk sneaking off to the pond for a drink and perhaps find a bite to eat, two of the colony beavers came over the hill toward him.

He said nothing and continued working. They just stood there above him and watched. At last one of them spoke.

"This project is taking much longer than we had thought. Do you have an explanation?"

Michael was so angry that he felt like picking up one of those rocks he had just dug up and throwing it at them. But he didn't. They wanted to know whether he had an explanation. He had a thousand explanations.

Why didn't they feed him better? Then he'd be stronger and could work faster. Why didn't they make this a community project? With all the men and youth working together, this could have been finished long ago. And it would have been fun.

Did he have an explanation? Yes, he did! Why didn't they . . . ah, what was the use, they wouldn't understand. . . .

Suddenly he realized that they were standing on the bank of the dry canal above him, still waiting for his answer. He smiled and simply replied, "No, I have no explanation."

That was the moment when it happened! Later he remembered it as the exact moment when the thought, the absolutely wild and crazy thought, had hit him: *Quit and go home!*

He said nothing about this to anyone. For a few more days, he continued working. But all the time he was pushing earth, he was thinking of going home.

One day it seemed such a brilliant idea to him, but the next day he wasn't so sure. One moment he thought that he had at last come to his senses, and the next moment he thought he was out of his mind.

A thousand thoughts raced through his head: It's all my fault. I wanted to leave home; I was not sent away. I wanted to see the world, to have fun. I didn't want to work all the time. I wanted to do things my way. I asked for my part of the inheritance, and I got it. Now it's gone, trashed, wasted.

Usually when he got that far in his thinking, he became so discouraged at the thought of going home. How could he possibly face his father? How could he explain what he had done with all the inheritance his father had given him?

The next day, the thoughts would be there again. Thoughts about himself, his hunger, his loneliness, but also thoughts about his father. He began to think more and more about his father. How would he meet him? What would he say? Would his father take him back?

As time went on, Michael began to talk to himself. He was actually making little speeches. They were always the same. He imagined that he had arrived at home, he had met his father, and he was kneeling in front of him. Michael tried out what he would say.

"Father, I did a terrible thing! I made a fool of myself. I brought shame on you. I have no right to be your son. But if you'll take me back, I'd be ever so thankful just to work for you as a hired paw."

He looked up, and there were the two boss beavers from the colony, standing on the bank of the dry canal bed, looking down on him. They had heard some of his little speech. Instantly Michael jumped to his feet, turned around, and started to work.

"Is that why it's taking you so long to get this canal done?" one of them asked in a voice as cold as ice. "Who were you talking to? Is that what you do here all day, kneel in the canal and make pretty speeches?"

The next day when the community leaders came to inspect the progress of the canal, Michael was not there. He was gone. They looked for him everywhere but could not find him.

Michael had left no message, and they had no idea where he had gone or when he would be back. They didn't know that they would never see him again.

The trip home seemed much shorter and faster than away from home. The closer Michael got to his familiar lake, the more often he stopped to go over the speech he was going to make to his father.

The more he repeated it, the more he wondered whether his father would actually take him back, even as a hired paw. Sometimes he changed the words, but no matter how he worded it, the message was always the same: "I'm sorry! Please take me back!"

The last time he had tried those words, everything was so real to him. He realized that he had been blind, foolish, stubborn, going his own way—yes, especially that, having his own way! He had wasted his inheritance and hurt his father.

When all that hit him, he moaned, "I'm sorry!" and burst out crying. He threw himself on the ground and wept bitterly. That time he didn't finish the speech. He only got as far as, "Father, I'm sorry...."

There had been no word between him and his home since he had left. What Michael did not know and could not know was that his father never stopped loving him. And his father was quite sure that one day his son would come home again. As the days and weeks turned into months, this feeling grew stronger until he could hardly stand it any more.

Every evening just before sunset, Sam saw his father paddle out to the bank, climb to one of the highest spots, and look for a long time, always in the same direction. Sam knew he was gazing toward the way Michael took when he left.

Although his father never talked to Sam about it, he knew his dad was waiting for Michael to come home. When the sun got low and began to shine in his eyes, he'd lift a front paw to shield them from the glare.

Then Sam could see him wipe a tear from his eye, and he knew the tear was not from looking into the sun. When the sun had set and it got too dark to see, he'd come back home.

Sam was slightly amused and a bit irritated by his father's watching and waiting. One day he gently asked about his father's daily waiting. Did he really think Michael would come back?

"Oh, but he will, he will!" Father Beaver exclaimed instantly, with deep feeling. He was so sure.

"And I suppose you'll take him back?" Sam was

trying to hide his displeasure. "By the way, on what conditions would you take him back?"

"Conditions?" repeated his father as if he hadn't understood. "Conditions? You ask what conditions. I hadn't thought about any conditions."

"Well, that's just like you," griped Sam. "With all due respect, Father, if you ask me, I think in the first place, Michael won't come back. But if he does, you should lay down the law. Make him promise a thing or two. You know, have him make up for what he's done!"

"Sam, I don't think you understand. I see it this way. In the first place, Michael left of his own free will. If he comes back, it will be of his own free will. I will not make him come back!"

"But you would take him back?" Now Sam was showing that he was annoyed. "After all he has done to you? After the disgrace he brought on our family, you would take him back without any conditions?"

"Of course I would." The father smiled broadly. "If you are puzzled about this, Sam, it's because there are two words in our language that you don't seem to understand. The words are *love* and *forgive*."

Sam didn't have anything more to say. He was just about to leave when he turned to his father and objected, "But what about two other words, like *justice* and *punish?* Aren't they also part of Beaver law and tradition?"

Meanwhile, Michael kept pushing on. Exactly nine months after leaving home, he arrived on the opposite bank of his lake. In the distance he could see the round tops of the houses, his own community. Now he was on the homestretch. This time no motorboat or water snake could scare him or stop him. His heart pounded with excitement.

He stretched out on the green grass to rest and to collect his mind. He'd have to spend the night here, but the next day would be his last away from home. By evening he should be there.

When Michael thought about home, a soft smile came over his face. Slowly the smile faded into a worried look. For a brief moment, there was even fear in his eyes. The outside showed what was inside, mixed-up thoughts and feelings.

Michael knew what he had to do: recite his speech. At the moment, that was the most important thing, to make sure he knew all the words and gave them in the right tone. His speech was brief, but it said everything that he wanted to say when he met his father.

As Michael repeated it once more, for the last time, he realized that he had not memorized the words to be spoken as an actor speaks words on a stage. Instead, they were his own words. Every one of the words came from the depths of his own heart. He meant every word he was going to say.

If only his father would let him say them! If he would listen to Michael. If only he would believe him. If only he would not throw him out before he could make his statement: "Father, I'm sorry! Please forgive me." But he wanted to be sure he also got to say that he was ready be a hired paw instead of a son.

Never had there been a beaver that swam so sure and so fast as Michael the next morning when he plunged into the lake and set off for home. Never had there been a father longing so much to see his son again as on that evening when Father Beaver climbed to his familiar perch to take a long look across the lake into the sunset.

Then it all happened fast. Father Beaver ran to meet him. Michael swam to the shore, climbed up the bank, and fell on his knees before his father. He began his speech: "Father, I'm sorry, please forgive me. . . ." But that's as far as he got.

Later Michael was telling his father that he had wanted to say more but hadn't had a chance. His father looked puzzled. He wondered why Michael hadn't finished his speech. What was it that he had wanted to say but didn't?

"I was going to say that I was not good enough to be your son," stated Michael. "Then I was going to ask you to take me on as a hired paw."

"I know why you didn't say that," said a friend standing beside the two and listening to their happy conversation. "I watched you both and heard every word that was spoken. The reason you didn't say those words, Michael, is because it is hard to speak when someone is hugging and kissing you all the time."

"Is that what I was doing?" Father Beaver was surprised and laughing. "Was I kissing Michael in the middle of his speech?"

"Yes, indeed, Father," Michael told him. "That's why I couldn't talk and finish what I was going to say."

Michael threw himself on the ground and wept bitterly.

They all laughed and then started another round of hugs and kisses.

Meanwhile, the news spread fast that Michael was back and his father was having a feast for him. Everyone seemed to know it except Sam, the older brother. He was far away on the lake with one of his construction projects and didn't get home till late that evening.

"What's that music coming from our house?" he asked a neighbor. "Sounds like dance music. And why are so many beavers all over our place?"

"Sam, we have the best news you can imagine!" His friend was beaming. "Michael is back! That's right, Michael, your runaway, no-good brother turned up again, late this afternoon. And is your father ever happy! Right now they're about to sit down to a huge dinner of all kinds of good food!"

The longer Sam listened, the less he liked what he heard. He wanted to have nothing to do with these celebrations. Suddenly, without saying anything, he turned around and left, with bitter thoughts.

A good licking is what Michael deserved, not a banquet. How could his father be so blind? Didn't he see what was happening? Didn't he know how Michael had disgraced their good family name? How he'd made a fool of himself? In fact, wasn't his father making a fool of himself, too, at this very moment?

Sam was still sulking and mumbling to himself when his father swam up alongside of him by the half-finished dam. After a few moments of silence, Father Beaver began.

"I think I know how you feel, Sam, but look at it this way. Your brother was lost, and now he is found. No, he wasn't lost in a sense that he didn't know where he was, but he surely was lost in the sense that he was all mixed up. You know that.

"He thought he'd be happy if he could just have his own way. Well, he had it. He found out the hard way that swimming by yourself doesn't make you happy. Now he's back. He's home again. Isn't that wonderful!"

"For him, yes," replied Sam curtly. "He got his way going, and now he gets his way coming. For me, there's nothing wonderful about it."

"Why Sam, what do you mean? I don't understand."

"Just listen to that music," complained Sam. "They're dancing. They're eating. When did I ever get to do that with my friends?"

"But why didn't you, Sam? Is it perhaps because you're always working? You know that everything I have is yours."

Sam didn't say anything. Suddenly this older brother felt like saying good-bye and leaving the home place. He was so disgusted, he felt like kicking somebody.

"Why don't you come in," pleaded his father. "Come and say hi to Michael. Meet his friends. Have some food. Join the party, Michael's homecoming party."

Sam's flat tail hit the water with a terrible smack. "Not in a thousand years, I won't. I'll have nothing to do with that no-good son of yours!" he snapped.

"But what about forgiving him?" asked his father. "Look what our welcome has done for Michael. He's like a new person. And it certainly has made *me* happy. I think there's nothing greater than forgiving."

Sam's eyes were cold and hard. "What about a little justice, Father? Why don't you punish him? What about that garbage . . . that evil he's done? Are you going to sweep it all under the rug?"

"Listen my son, he did a lot of wrong, but he knows it, and he's sorry for it. That's why he came home. The purpose of punishment is to make you see that you've done wrong. Punishment is to make you repent. But Michael has already done that. So why punish him now? What for?"

"To teach him a lesson," barked Sam, "that's why!"

"But he's already learned the lesson," pleaded his father. "He's dreadfully sorry about the way he messed things up. He told me so. And coming back is proof of it."

There was a long silence. Father Beaver began to realize that he had found his younger son but was about to lose his older son. What should he do? He could command Sam to come in. Obedient as he was, he'd probably do it. But then what? It just wasn't the way he did things.

When Michael had wanted to leave home, he had let him go. When he was gone, he didn't make him come back. So now he wasn't going to make Sam come into the house and join the party. One was as free to do or not to do as the other.

At last he said, "Listen to how happy they are.

You, too, would be happy if you would come in. Why don't you think about it?"

"He can keep his happiness!" growled Sam. "I'm not going in!" Again he smacked the water with his flat tail so it splashed in every direction.

For the same reason that he had let his younger son leave home, the Father now left the older son outside, to do as he pleased. He would not force either of them.

Slowly he turned around and swam back to the house, to the music and the food, the dancing and the laughing. Back to his son—the son who had come home again.

To compare this with the original story, read Luke 15:11-32.

"The long and the short of it," figured Fanny Fox about the afternoon's story. "It was a long story and a short afternoon. Time just seemed to fly, as it always does when a story is that good."

"The older brother couldn't do anything but work," Billy Raccoon commented. "A bit dull, don't you think?"

"Maybe. But he obeyed the rules," responded Fanny. "His father didn't criticize him for that."

"But to think that the father just took back that racing-around spendthrift without punishing him!" exclaimed Billy. "That's really something. I guess that's what it means to forgive. He wouldn't even hear of making him a hired paw."

"If you ask me," Fanny added, "I think that's super. If you put the two facts together, it makes sense."

"What two facts?" asked Billy.

"That the father loved his son, and that the son was sorry for the way he'd messed things up."

"Talking of being sorry," added Billy, "I couldn't help feeling sorry for the older fellow, the good guy."

"Sorry, yes," agreed Fanny. "But was he a good guy? Oh, by the way, I've heard that tonight's story is about good guys and bad guys. We don't want to miss that."

Again Rabbit was up on his fallen tree, waving for everyone to come closer. He didn't really have to do that because the animals were streaming to the meeting by the hundreds and going right up to the front. As soon as they had settled themselves comfortably on the grass, Rabbit began.

"A few minutes ago I asked Mother Muskrat what her story tonight was about, and she said 'good guys and bad guys.' She wouldn't tell me more. I guess we'll just have to wait till we hear it. I am pleased to call on the storyteller of the evening, our own beloved Mother Muskrat."

She climbed up beside Rabbit, stood up, and began. "I will let you decide who's a good guy and who's a bad guy. Just let me tell the story. But one thing you should know before I start. In the story, the person I call 'Mother Muskrat' is not me. She was my great-grandmother."

Evening: Muskrat's Story

Now Who's the Good Guy?

Mother Muskrat came out of the water, climbed to the round roof of her house, and looked around her marsh. As far as she could see, things were calm.

Nearby where the marsh joined the lake, the shore was quiet. She could see no hunters with guns. There were no noisy motorboats. The weather was balmy. It seemed like a perfect day for her children to be out for a swim.

"How beautiful they are," she thought as she watched them getting ready. Stroking the dark brown fur of the smallest one, Musky number six, she tickled his tiny ears, hardly sticking up above his glossy hair.

"Here, let me take a look at your tail," she said to Musky number three. It was flat and stubby, the way it ought to be. But the part covered with scales instead of hair seemed to be scuffed. "What happened, honey?" she asked in the concerned voice of mothers everywhere. "Did you get hurt?"

"Just a bit," replied the little fellow. "It happened yesterday when we were out. Something got hold of my tail, but I jerked away."

"That's a big boy!" she praised him. "But please be careful, all of you. And stay away from the Bruce gang. They're a bad lot."

"You always say that, Mother," griped Musky number five. "Why are they a bad lot? You've never told us."

"Because they're no good, that's why! They've always been bad. Now swim along and enjoy yourselves."

Musky number one jumped off the roof of their mound-house and dived straight into the water with a splash. Muskies numbers two and three slid gracefully down the side and then paddled away. The other two preferred the conventional way of scampering down inside their mound-house and slipping out through the underwater door.

Father Pavel came up to the roof to join Mother Muskrat just in time to see the last two pop out of the water and join the others. Pavel and Mother Muskrat waved to them as they started to swim away together.

"Don't have anything to do with the Bruce children," Father Pavel called after them. Then the Muskrat parents stretched out for a little rest as they watched their children frolic and splash.

"Why do we always tell them to stay away from the Bruce children?" asked Mother Muskrat. "I had just told them that before you came."

"You know why." Father Pavel was slightly irritated. "They're no good, that's why. We don't want them to make our children no good. It's just best to avoid them."

"I don't mean to be difficult," continued Mother Muskrat, "but I would like to understand the problem. Then I could explain it to the children. They keep asking me why they have to stay away from the Bruces."

"You *are* a bit difficult." Father Pavel had a snap of anger in his voice. "You well know what happened long ago. Don't you remember that they went off and became a separate bunch? Yes, a separate bunch and a bad bunch!"

"I don't want to annoy you," Mother Muskrat added kindly, "but that's what everybody keeps saying: 'They're a bad bunch' and 'You know what happened.' All right, so they went off and became a separate clan. But why? What was so bad about that? Frankly, I don't know what happened, and I just don't understand. That's why I'm asking."

Father Pavel changed his voice and gave his wife a faint smile. "That's a long story, and it happened a long time ago. They moved away from us, or we moved away from them, I don't exactly know. It doesn't matter.

"They're strange. They have their territory, and we have ours. They're not even at the edge of the lake, like we are, with fresh water all around. Where they live, it's all marsh. Their water is shallow and murky, more like a swamp. I wouldn't be surprised if it stinks."

He paused a moment and then added with a

sneer, "And they stink too. All of them!"

Father Pavel looked at the sun and then at the direction of his shadow. Suddenly he put his brown paw on hers and in a changed mood announced cheerfully, "Well, it's time I was off! I'll see you after the meeting."

He scampered below to use the underwater exit. Before he came up on the surface outside, Mother Muskrat thought about what he had just told her. She hadn't heard one thing new. In fact, he had not really explained why the Bruce Muskrats were a bad bunch.

Father Pavel had simply repeated what she had heard all her life: "It happened a long time ago. They're no good! Stay away from them! Don't go into their territory. Don't even talk to them! Have nothing to do with them!" And now the latest: "They stink!"

Meanwhile Father Pavel was swimming along making good time. With his webbed five-toed hind legs, he pushed ahead, grumbling as he went. The conversation with his wife about the Bruces had upset him. He knew that he hadn't given her much of an answer. Her question was perfectly reasonable.

The problem was, he didn't know himself why the Bruces were such a bad bunch. Except that they were. That's what he had been told ever since he could remember. He'd never seen one or talked to one himself.

Gradually his mood changed as he realized how glad he was not to be a Bruce Muskrat. How awful it must be to be one of them! How wonderful to be the leader of the Pavel Muskrats! He and his tribe were wonderful. Not perfect, but a good bunch of Muskrats. And so were the Lowells. One could depend on them. It was a joy to be together with them in the same lake.

Suddenly he saw something up ahead that made him slow down. Since he could swim as well under water as on the surface, he had to make a quick decision. Should he go under and pass the object unnoticed, or stay on the surface and see what it was. He was curious, so he decided to stay on top. He slowed down as he came closer.

What is it? he thought. It looks like a piece of floating driftwood. But wait, driftwood doesn't make sounds. He listened, and there it was again, a faint groan. Whatever it was, the "thing" was alive. He'd better be careful.

Slowly and silently he moved closer. Soon he saw it. It was a muskrat. Poor fellow! He seemed to have had an accident of some kind. The water around him was stained red. He must be bleeding, thought Father Pavel. Perhaps someone had attacked him. He was groaning, in pain. Somebody ought to do something for the poor fellow, he thought. He needs help.

Just then an idea hit Father Pavel. What if the bad guy who had hurt the poor fellow was coming back to finish him off? Or what if he was just lurking below the surface less than a hundred feet away, ready at any moment to kill both of them?

A shiver ran down his spine. He did not want to get himself killed. Today he had a meeting to attend, and a family to think of. So, wasting no more time, he streaked away on the double.

Meanwhile, Lewis and his wife were saying good-bye to each other in the new style they had recently developed—swimming together and chatting for while before separating. They had swum side by side for at least five hundred yards when she murmured, "I'm proud of you, Lewis." She reached over and stroked his smooth, wet fur. It was dark brown and glossy. She admired him and the way his fur shone in the sun.

"And I love you," he responded as he playfully splashed water over her tiny ears and beady eyes. "We Muskrats have compact and chubby bodies, but do I notice that yours is getting more round than usual?" Laughter was in his voice.

"You're very observant." She smiled. "And now you know why I have trouble keeping up with you."

"Oh, happy day!" shouted Father Lewis. "When is the big event? How many babies do you think there will be this time?"

She didn't answer. Suddenly she turned to him and asked, "Is it true that the Bruce Muskrats are as bad as we hear they are?"

Lewis slowed down almost to a stop. Spreading his tail on the water for balance, he just floated as he looked at his pregnant wife and replied solemnly, "They *are* a bad lot. There's not a good Muskrat among them. You never saw anyone as mean as the Bruces."

"Have you ever seen one? Do you actually know a Bruce in person?"

"Not really," he confessed. "But look, everybody

knows it. They couldn't all be wrong. What's more, it's been like that ever since I can remember."

"Tell me about them. Why are they no good?"

"Why are they no good?" Lewis repeated like an echo. "Because they aren't, that's why. It's a long story. It happened a long time ago. They went away, or we went away. I don't really know who went first. And I don't think I know why. But they've always been separate. They're a lowdown bunch of critters."

He kissed her good-bye and was off. Slowly she returned to their mound-home, thinking, He didn't tell me anything. I don't think he knows. And he never met a Bruce Muskrat himself? He's just repeating what he's heard others say since he was little.

Lewis was a good swimmer. Whether under water or on top made no difference to him. In no time he had gone so far that his mound had faded in the distance. But he hadn't forgotten the discussion with his wife.

I wonder why she asked about the Bruces, he thought. I hope I'll never meet one as long as I live.

He was happy to be a Lewis Muskrat, happy to be their leader. They were a good bunch. Solid and dependable. Always kept the rules. That was important, keeping the rules.

As he swam along, he kept thinking about his own Muskrats, the Lewis bunch, as they were named. Sometimes they were also called the Rules Muskrats. That was alright with him. Every family and every community had to have rules. Without rules, there would be no living together.

Life would be chaos. It would be a jungle.

Suddenly he saw something up ahead that required all his attention. He stopped thinking about rules, about his wife, and about what a good bunch of Muskrats his Lewises were. He focused all his attention on the dark object floating on the water. Experience had taught him to be careful in unusual situations. This could be a trick. There might be danger.

Slowly he approached the object. He looked carefully and discovered that the object was not a thing at all, as he had thought. While he was watching, he noticed that it moved a bit. He heard it groan. And then he saw it clearly. It was a muskrat. The poor fellow seemed to be in trouble. He was bleeding and the water all around him was stained red. The poor chap must be suffering and in pain.

Suddenly a word flashed into Lewis's mind. A brief four-letter word. He could see it as plainly as if it had been written out for him. It had been drilled into him all his life. The word was "rule." Live by the rules. Rules are made to guide life. Without rules, life is a jungle. Always live by the rules, especially in an emergency.

All this flashed through his mind faster than he could blink an eye. Equally fast, rule number three came to mind: "When it's none of your business, keep your paws off!"

Lewis started to back off. He could hear the groaning, and he saw the poor fellow twitch with pain. But what business of his was this accident or mugging or whatever it was? He just happened to come along. That was all.

He hadn't done it, didn't know who had done it, didn't even know what had been done or why. He didn't know anything, really. In fact, he didn't even know the muskrat in trouble. This was none of his business!

He was still thinking these thoughts when rule number two flashed on the screen of his mind: "Always look out for number one." He remembered his grandfather telling him that the instinct to preserve self was the most important of all the gifts that the Great Spirit had given to muskrats. If it hadn't been for that, there wouldn't be any muskrats alive today.

Quite sure that he was doing the right thing, Lewis swam on and left the wounded muskrat behind. On the one hand he was sorry for the suffering victim. But on the other, he was happy that he had been taught the rules of life and how to apply them in every situation. "Good guys always live by the rules," he muttered to himself. "Right here is a case in point: If the bad guys had lived by the rules, there wouldn't have been this mugging in the first place."

Meanwhile, off in the distance and back where the water was shallow and murky, Bruce said he had business on the other side of the lake. He hugged his wife and kids good-bye and promised that he would be back in several days.

• • •

Much later that day, another scene took place. Pavel's wife was excited when she met her neighbor. "Did you hear what happened today? The whole community is talking about it."

Muskrats were coming from every direction. Even before they reached the Pavel mound, they began to ask questions. Everybody wanted to know what had happened. They all had heard something, but none of them were able to put the whole story together.

"There was a mugging," reported one of the muskrats. "A cruel and bloody affair."

"Pavel will be home soon. Maybe he can tell us about it," suggested Pavel's wife.

"I'm waiting for my husband, too," added Lewis's wife. "Maybe he knows something about it."

"I don't know what Pavel or Lewis saw, or whether they saw anything," said one of the muskrats. "But what I know, I know. And when I tell you, you won't believe it!"

They all turned to the speaker and recognized their friend Nestor, the man who had the only restaurant and marina in the area.

"Tell us, Nestor, please tell us!" begged a dozen or more voices at once. "What happened? And how come you know about it? Did you swim in that part of the lake today, too? Did you see the mugging?"

"No, I didn't. I was minding my own business when this stranger," he paused a moment as if hesitating to say it, but then continued, "when this stranger, this Bruce fellow, came swimming up to my marina. That's right, it was a Bruce muskrat. He came right up to my dock."

There were gasps of surprise and paws lifted up as if to ward off evil. Then someone in the crowd called out, "I hope you didn't let him in!"

Quick as that came another voice, "I bet he's the one who did it. What did you find out?"

"I found out that he wasn't alone," Nestor went on. "He was floating the mugged fellow along behind him, towing him by his tail. At first I thought he was dead, but it turned out there was still a little life left in him."

"A Bruce at your marina? Pulling that beat-up fellow behind him?" asked several voices in disbelief. "Are you putting us on?"

"You haven't heard anything yet," continued Nestor. "The Bruce had already given him some first aid before he brought him to me. You know, the usual things. But when he got to my motel on the marina, he didn't beg me to save the poor guy. He just expected me to help.

"You should have heard him. Not angry, mind you, not proud either, just sure and firm, as if he knew what he was doing. 'Help me bind up his wounds,' he simply stated. After we bandaged him up, he added, 'Now let's get him into a bed! And give him some food! Watch him until he gets better!'"

"Wow! And all the time you did what he told you to do?" asked the other muskrats.

"Of course I did. I really had no choice. I mean, in the first place, the poor fellow did need help. In the second place, that Bruce chap wasn't rough or unkind. He just knew what had to be done and did it. I mean, *we* did it.

"In the third place, just as soon as we had the worst taken care of and were cleaning up his scratches and doing some more bandaging, the Bruce began telling me about how he was going to make it all up to me."

"Make it up to you?" asked the muskrats in amazement. "How was he going to do that?"

"No problem. He said he had everything a muskrat needs for a good and happy life. I was to say what I needed for the expenses, the food, the nest, the bandages, the medicine, and all that. He'd pay me back. Just like that!"

There were more expressions of surprise and amazement. Some wanted to know what was in it for this Bruce fellow, since he was not only one of the bad guys but the leader of that rotten bunch. Why had he done this? What would move him to save a strange muskrat's life?

They all talked at once. Some were saying that perhaps the Bruces weren't as bad as they had been made out to be. Others were wondering why somebody else hadn't helped the beat-up fellow before Bruce came along.

Suddenly there was a splashing sound, and two more muskrats came out of the water to join the others. It was Pavel and Lewis. When they saw the crowd and heard what the discussion was about, they didn't say anything. Pavel started grooming his fur, and Lewis made as if he wanted to go home. There was a long silence. Everybody expected them to say something.

Presently two women, the wives of Pavel and Lewis, moved over to their husbands, put their paws on their shoulders and whispered something into their ears.

Everyone watched this unusual greeting. They all wondered what they had told them or asked them? What would the two leaders say?

As they waited, Pavel and Lewis became serious. Instead of speaking to everyone there, they only muttered to their wives something that sounded like "Yes, we know" and "You're right!"

What was it that they knew? What did they agree with when they told their wives that they were right? Everybody wanted to know.

In the last faint whispers, they could only make out two words. All the rest was a mumbled blur. But they did hear the two women say the words "Bruce" and "neighbor" several times. They didn't know what "neighbor" had to do with Bruce or the mugged muskrat.

Everybody looked at everybody else. Neither Pavel nor Lewis seemed to have anything to say. When they left, the others shrugged their shoulders and finally drifted away, too. They swam to their own homes, hoping that later they would find out what the bad guy Bruce had to do with *neighbor.*

Whose neighbor?

If you want a shorter and more original version of this story, read Luke 10:29-37.

"If you ask me," said one of the youngsters discussing the story of the evening, "those muskrats living in the swamp didn't stink. The stink came from the 'good' guys like Pavel and Lewis, living in the fresh water."

"True. True," agreed a number of kids at once. "The really good guy was a Bruce. He helped the wounded beaver."

"That story wasn't so long. Shall we ask Brother Beaver for a short bedtime tale?" asked one of the girls.

"There he goes. Run and bring him here!" squealed another. "And don't take no for an answer."

Moments later, Timmy had outrun all the others and came back with Brother Beaver.

"So it's another story you want." He smiled and settled down in the grass with the group of young people. "This is becoming a habit. After the three stories of the day, another short one off in a corner somewhere. Especially for the young ones."

"Please, just a short tale," they begged. "You're the best storyteller around."

"Flattery will get you nowhere," Beaver laughed. "But I do love youngsters, and I do love to tell stories. I think I'll tell you another one about two beaver brothers. They happened to be my cousins. This story is not on the program for the day, yet it is true. Let me simply call the story by the names of the two boys, Burly and Blinky.

Bedtime: Beaver's Story 4

Burly and Blinky

They had been splashing about in the lake all morning. The water was cool and clear, reflecting a white cloud slowly drifting in the sky. It was a perfect morning for diving, racing, and just frolicking about.

"Burly, come over here, please!" came a voice across the water. They both recognized it at once.

"Father is calling you," yelled Blinky, his brother. "You better go and see what he wants."

"Why always me?" grumbled Burly. "I wouldn't be surprised if he had another job for me to do. When he calls like that, it usually means our fun is over."

"Come on, why don't we both go and see what Dad wants?" Blinky leaped out of the water, shouting, "Let's race!" and came down with a nosedive, disappearing under the water for a minute or two.

Then he streaked along on the surface with Burly close behind and catching up with him. They were both out of breath when they came to a stop in front of their father.

"You're both excellent swimmers," complimented Father Beaver. "Burly, you're a little faster, but that's because you're older than Blinky. You're older so you're stronger. But you did well, Blinky."

Father Beaver smiled at his two sons. He was proud of them. They were good lads, with the promise of one day becoming trusted leaders in the Beaver Colony.

To start them off early in training to be leaders and handle problems, Father Beaver gave each of them jobs to do from time to time. He praised them when they did the work willingly and well and corrected them when they were grumpy or did a sloppy job.

"I have to go to the other side of the lake this morning," Father Beaver began. "It's an important meeting with beavers from other parts of the lake. But it's a bad time for me to leave because we are almost finished building this dam."

Burly and Blinky looked at each other but said nothing. They knew all about building dams. They knew exactly what their father was talking about. If a beaver leaves a dam unfinished, in no time at all the water pushing against it and flowing over it might wash it away. Once someone started building, it was best to complete it as quickly as possible.

"So I was thinking, Burly, that you could be the dam-building engineer until I come back. You're the oldest and strongest, and you have more experience than Blinky. Perhaps you'll even have it finished by the time I get back. It'll be late tonight. The moon will be up by the time I come home."

"Didn't I tell you, Blinky? That call meant there's work to do," grumbled Burly. "And it's always me. 'Burly, do this,' and 'Burly, do that.' "

"Because you're the oldest and strongest," repeated Father Beaver. "You know we can't leave the dam like this. The last few logs are already cut and need to be floated into position now and weighted down with rocks. The branches and sticks must be glued in place with mud to hold everything together.

"If that isn't done, you know there might not be much left of the dam by the time I get back. Try to roll an extra log on top to tie it together and to give us the safety of a little more water around our mounds."

"Ya, ya, we know all that!" grumbled Burly in a sassy voice. "You always ask us to do some work just when we're having a good time in the lake. This time I just won't do it."

Blinky was surprised at his brother's attitude. He didn't like the way he talked to his father. Now he was sure there was going to be trouble. Blinky knew that Father Beaver could be strict when necessary.

To prevent a logjam between his father and brother, Blinky did something noble, a complete surprise for the other two. He even surprised himself.

"I'll finish building the dam!" he offered. "I know how to do it. It will take me longer to finish building it than if Burly did it, but I can do it.

Please, Dad, let me work on the dam."

Burly said nothing. He had not expected his younger brother to volunteer for the job. But if Blinky wanted to do it, let him.

"That's wonderful!" responded Father Beaver. "I was really hoping that the two of you could work together with Burly as the engineer. But of course, you can do it yourself.

"It doesn't matter if it takes a bit longer. Just so you do it well. Remember, always do the best you can. Don't be careless. A slipshod job has to be done over again. It's time and energy wasted. On top of that, it gives you a bad reputation."

"I know." Blinky smiled at his Father. "You've told us that many times. I'll do the best I can. I'll just get a quick bite to eat, and then I'll start working. When you come back, the dam will be finished."

Father Beaver laid a paw on Blinky's shoulder. "Good boy! I'm proud of you."

He looked at Burly. He didn't know what to say. Scolding him would do no good. It might make matters worse. Perhaps he just ought to let it go without any more words.

After all, Burly knew better than to let an unfinished dam go to pieces and float away. He certainly knew better than to disobey his father. This was the first time he'd done that. They would have to talk about it, but not now. Father Beaver decided he would go to his meeting and talk to Burly the next day.

Late that morning, Burly happened to look out over the lake and saw a young beaver splashing about. He seemed to be having a lot of fun. But Burly was in no mood for fun and frolic. He was brooding, going over in his mind for the tenth time the conversation between his father and himself that morning.

"That was a stupid thing I did," he muttered to himself. "My father had every right to ask me to finish building that dam. Some son I am! I sure hurt him.

"Father was actually doing me a favor by giving me his work to finish. He trusted me. He gave me responsibility.

"Later he could say to his friends, 'See that dam over there? We started it together, but my son Burly finished it!' Boy, was I ever dumb. I really blew it."

Burly was thinking these thoughts and idly looking out over the lake. Then he saw again in the distance that young beaver splashing about and having a lot of fun all by himself.

Now he noticed a special kind of jump out of the water, a dive under the surface, and moments later a fast streaking away. Where had he seen that before? It seemed familiar.

Within minutes Burly was out beside the frolicking beaver. He was right. It *was* his brother.

"Blinky, what are you doing here?" asked Burly. "I thought you were working on the dam."

"What dam?" Blinky joked, pretending he didn't know. "Did you see that last jump I made? I'm really getting good!"

"Good at what?" asked Burly in surprise. "Jumping or working? You promised Dad that you would work on the dam. He believed you. Now what's this about?"

"Of course he believed me because I meant it. I really did. It seemed such a good idea at the moment, especially when I saw you and Dad at loggerheads. But later, well. . . ."

"Well, what?" prompted Burly, who wanted to hear the rest of the sentence. "Why didn't you go to work the way you said you would?"

"Well, you know. . . ."

"No, I don't know. Suppose you tell me. All I know is that I told Dad I wasn't going to do it, and you told him you *were* going to do it."

"Well, that's just it," continued Blinky. "I thought that if you didn't want to work, why should I? Besides, this is such a good time for practicing some of my leaps and dives. So. . . ."

"So just like that, you broke your promise, is that it?"

"That's not fair, pushing me like that. You didn't want to work either," snapped Blinky, annoyed at his older brother. "I'm in no more trouble than you are."

Burly didn't say any more. He gave his brother a long look, then turned and swam away. He paddled in the direction of the dam.

Blinky also swam away, out to the middle of the lake. Burly could hear him splashing and squealing with delight as he practiced his leaps and dives.

Father Beaver came home late, just after the moon had risen. Before entering their family home, he swam out to take a quick look at the dam. It was all finished. He decided to inspect it more carefully first thing in the morning.

He entered his home, found his bed, and lay down to sleep. He looked over to the other side of the room and saw his two sons fast asleep. Then he remembered that in the morning, he would have to talk to Burly. He didn't look forward to that. But he knew that it was a father's responsibility to do that.

He didn't know that a surprise was waiting for him. He didn't know that the one who had said he would do it did not do it; and the one who said he would not do it did it!

You may see how Matthew told this story in 21:28-31.

Third Day

"This is the last day of our jamboree," observed Myrtle the Turtle the next morning. "Three more stories, and we'll be on our way home."

"But what a jamboree this is! We'll be talking about it all the way home and for days to come. We don't want to forget these stories," replied Marcia the Margay.

"Have you noticed how the children and grown-ups come and listen?" asked Myrtle. "I am so glad I came. We must have another jamboree next year."

"Yes! Yes! Yes!" agreed Marcia. "And three days is just the right length of time, too. But look, they're going to the meeting. Let's hurry so we get good seats."

Rabbit was having fun with somebody up on his fallen tree, his platform. From a distance Myrtle and Marcia had trouble making out who was up there with Rabbit. Then they saw clearly that it was a duck.

"Your attention, please!" called Rabbit. "Quiet, everybody! This morning we have a special treat. Our storyteller is none other than Grandmother Dorothy Duck. She has an exciting story to share with us, a story told in her family for many generations.

"I asked her for the title, but I don't think I understand. It's something about a double-yolked egg. We rabbits know almost nothing about eggs. I haven't a clue as to what a double-yolked egg is. So let's give our full attention to Dorothy."

Dorothy Duck raised herself up and quacked a few times the way ducks do. "I hope you can understand my bird language. I'll speak slowly and distinctly. It's a bit different from animal language, but if you listen carefully, you'll soon catch on."

Everybody applauded. It was clear that they already understood her.

"Rabbit heard me correctly," she continued. "My story title is 'The Double-yolked Egg.'

"Don't worry about eggs not being part of your animal experience. You'll soon find out that whether we are covered by feathers or fur, inside we are not very different. We all have feelings of love and hate, envy and pride, sadness and joy."

Dorothy Duck paused a moment and looked over her large audience. She saw all the youngsters up front, gave them a broad smile, and then continued.

"My story is about my two great-uncles, Emery and Jason. Or maybe they were my great-great-uncles. They lived a long time ago, but we know exactly what kind of persons they were and what they did.

"You see, in our Duck clan, we have a tradition of passing on true family tales from one generation to another. And this is the story."

Morning: Duck's Story

The Double-yolked Egg

One bright Saturday morning, a duck named Hakeber sat on her nest the way all ducks do when they hatch their eggs.

"Tomorrow we can expect the ducklings to break through the shell," she announced proudly when Drake, her husband, asked how she was doing.

"How can you be so sure?" he teased. "Maybe it'll be another week."

"Nonsense!" His wife laughed. "Another week would make it five weeks. Eaglets hatch in six weeks or so, not ducklings. We hatch in thirty days."

"You're a clever wife to know all that."

"Not really. When I sit on this nest, I have a lot of time to think. For example, I think why my distant cousin, the sparrow, hatches her eggs in fourteen days; why my closer cousin, the hen, hatches hers in twenty-one days; why mine hatch in thirty days; why the eagle hatches hers in six to eight weeks; and so on."

"Always about a week different—is that what you're saying?" asked Drake. "Never thought of that before."

"I don't think it just happened," stated Hakeber. "Someone planned it that way. Tomorrow is the thirtieth day that I've been sitting here, keeping this huge egg warm. Since I'm a duck and not a hen or an eagle, it will hatch tomorrow. Come around and celebrate. The egg will be broken, I assure you, and there will be ducklings!"

"I'll be here," promised Drake, her husband. "But isn't it strange that you have only one big egg this time? You seem to be sure that it is double-yolked. What do you think will happen when that hatches? Or maybe it won't hatch."

"Oh yes, it'll hatch all right. We'll have twins." Hakeber laughed again. "The first twins in our family." Her smile faded, and a cloud seemed to cast a shadow over her lovely face. After a moment of silence, she continued rather seriously.

"You know, Drake, they're not hatched yet, and already I'm worried."

"Why?" asked Drake. "Twins or singles, we'll manage. We always see that they get food, learn to swim, and stay safe."

"That's not what I'm worried about. We don't need to teach them how to swim. You know that. They'll swim the moment they crawl out of the shell. What worries me is that yesterday I felt that big egg move again."

"Is that so unusual?" asked Drake. "I remember you saying that a few days before ducklings hatch, there usually is some movement."

"That's right, my dear," replied Hakeber. "During the last hatching days, the duckling moves because it changes its position. That's a sign of life and good health, really. If the egg doesn't move, I roll it over myself from time to time.

"But this was no ordinary movement, and it wasn't the first time, either. I jumped off the nest for a bit and watched. That big egg moved first one way and then another, in short and jerky motions. I don't like to think this and even less to say it, but it almost seemed as if the twins inside were fighting."

"Now you're imagining things," quacked Drake reassuringly. "Just wait till they're hatched. They'll probably pop out of that shell cuddling each other."

"It would be nice," agreed Hakeber. "But the way the egg moved, it seemed more like struggle than hugging."

"Let's worry about that later," comforted Drake. "Now we must keep our eyes open. You know how important it is to know which one hatches first."

"I've been thinking about that, too," agreed Hakeber. "The first one out will be the oldest, and the oldest becomes the leader. He gets more of something. I don't know what it's called, but it's more of something—getting a promise, I think."

"I'll take care of that," declared Drake. "That is one thing I can do. It's my responsibility to take care of that. It's enough that you laid the egg and hatched it. You did a fine job. Just leave that Special Something to me. You're absolutely right. The oldest one, even if he is older by only a minute, gets the Special Something."

The next day Drake never left Hakeber and the egg. He either sat beside the nest watching her and the double-yolked egg, or he strolled around, but never more than a few waddles away.

He wanted to be right there to witness that important moment when the twins would hatch. He wanted to be sure he saw with his own eyes which duckling came out of the shell first.

"This is it!" whispered Hakeber, excited but still sitting on the eggs. "I can feel it now. They're coming out!" She moved away so Drake could witness the historic moment. They both sat beside the nest, watching.

The movement inside the big egg increased. It made a quarter roll to the right. Soon they noticed a little hole in the shell, no bigger than a pin prick.

"There's his beak coming through!" whispered Drake, at full attention. "Let's watch carefully now."

Both Drake and Hakeber felt like helping the little fellows get out. They could make the hole bigger from the outside, but they knew that was never done. They didn't quite know why it was not done.

Some said the duckling would die if you helped it out, but they didn't believe that. Others claimed the baby needed to exert itself and peck its own way into the world, or it would always be a weakling. Still others were sure that if it got help from the outside, it would always feel shy and depend on others too much. Whatever the real reason, both Hakeber and Drake didn't dare touch the egg.

They waited and watched as the hole got bigger. At one point they waited so long, they began to wonder whether something had gone wrong. They knew that sometimes ducklings used up their energy trying to break out of the shell and died in the last minute because all their strength had been spent. They had a special name for that.

"I hope it won't be a stillbirth," whispered Drake.

"No need to worry," Hakeber assured him. "They are healthy and strong. The way they've carried on lately, they're okay."

Just then the action started up again. All of a sudden, a large piece of shell broke away. Moments later another piece broke off. Suddenly the cutest little duckling popped out, a boy.

He looked around for a brief moment and wobbled a bit as he tried to steady himself on two legs. He rocked back and forth, a little uncertain, stretched its tiny wings, and turned its neck. That's when he saw the proud parents watching it.

"Hi! My name is Emery," he greeted them in duckling chirp. "You saw that I came out first."

Moments later his brother also crawled out of the broken egg. He had bits of shell sticking to him and couldn't keep his balance when he tried to stand.

Emery and Jason

"That's my brother, Jason," quacked Emery. "I had to break the shell for him or he wouldn't have made it."

Hakeber gave Drake a look that could have meant, I told you so. But then she turned to her newly hatched children.

"Welcome, both of you. We've been waiting a long time for you, and here you are. That's just great! And you both look fine!"

Emery didn't say another word. Without even taking a good look at his father or thanking his mother for having hatched him, he waddled away to hunt for food. Seeds, beetles, anything that looked appetizing and was bite-size was good enough. He hunted and ate until he was full.

When he came back, Jason was still sitting beside his mother, quacking all kinds of nonsense. Mostly he was telling her about how it had felt being inside the shell. Hakeber stroked his downy feathers, smiled, and quacked in a motherly way.

Just hatched, and already she's picked her favorite, thought Emery. But he didn't say a word. He pretended he hadn't noticed.

When they both laid down for their first afternoon nap, Emery gave his brother a sharp peck with his beak. Just when Jason was getting drowsy and going off to sleep, he gave him a shove that sent him flying out of the nest.

That afternoon the family went out together to explore the neighborhood. Emery walked with Drake, but Jason waddled along beside Hakeber. When they came to a small pond, Drake was about to tell Emery to be careful and let his dad show him how to swim. But Emery had already plunged into the water and was paddling around at a great rate.

Jason let himself down gently, close beside his mother. They all had a good time.

Soon it became clear that Father Drake liked Emery better than Jason. Whenever he wanted something special to eat, like his favorite co-le-OP-tera (beetles), he'd ask Emery to get them for him.

Emery would be out like a shot, hunting all over in the deep grass until he had found enough for a nice big meal. When he'd bring them home, he'd walk into the kitchen and see his brother, Jason, standing on tiptoe, watching his mother make mush from seeds. The two would be chatting away at a great rate.

One day when Emery and Jason happened to be alone in the field, Emery began teasing his brother the way he often did.

"Mama baby, mama baby," he quacked. "You're nothing but a mama baby."

"Go ahead, tease all you want," chirped Jason. "See if I care. You're just jealous, that's all!"

"Jealous of what?" snapped Emery. "Of being a mama baby?"

"Jealous that I can cook a meal in the kitchen and you can't!"

It was a weak response, and Jason knew it wasn't quite true. Perhaps Emery couldn't make a meal out of grain the way he could, but he certainly could prepare the beetles and bugs and other crawly things that he brought back from his hunting trips. His father loved the way he prepared them for him.

"Didn't I say you're a mama baby?" snarled Emery. "She even taught you how to cook seeds. Why don't you grow up and hunt for your food? Real food that has to be caught and killed.

"Why, you yellow-livered runt of a bird, I suppose you wouldn't know how to hunt. You don't even know how to kill." Emory made up a rhyme and sang it over and over.

> You're a runt and can't hunt,
> a runt and can't hunt,
> a runt and can't hunt.

Finally he stopped, waddled right up to his brother, and hissed into his face: "You're nothing but a mama baby! And a sissy, too."

Jason felt like biting his brother, Emery. He also felt like crying. But he didn't bite him and he didn't cry. He did what he always did when Emery upset him. He went home and told Hakeber everything Emery had done.

She stroked his feathers and let him crawl under her wings. There he'd feel safe and warm. Sometimes he went to sleep like that. Then he'd dream about getting even with his braggy, rough brother.

One day Emery had been out hunting all day but found nothing. At last it got too dark to hunt, and he had to come home. He was tired, thirsty, and absolutely famished. As he stumbled into the kitchen, Jason was just dishing out some seeds that he had cooked for his mother and himself.

"Give me some of that stuff," Emery demanded. "I'm so hungry, I could eat anything. Even your stupid mush."

Instantly Jason realized that this was the moment he'd been waiting for. For once his big brother was in trouble and needed him. He continued dishing out the boiled seeds, thinking fast, and pretending he hadn't heard him. The smell of the cooked food made Emery's mouth water.

"Are you going to give me that mush or not?" Emery quacked a second time. "I'm hungry."

"So I see," responded Jason. "Sure, I'll give it to you. All you can eat. But first you have to promise me something."

"Okay, spit it out. Just get on with it and don't keep me waiting. What do you want?"

"I want you to say that I came out of the shell first. That's all. Say that you came last."

"Well, it's not true, of course," griped Emery. "But if it makes you happy, sure I'll do that. Just give me something to eat or I'll faint."

"Oh, no, you won't," chirped Jason calmly. "It takes a lot more than that to faint. I want you to promise what I asked you, not just say it quickly and forget about it. I want you to vow it like promises made at a wedding."

"You're fussy! But who cares. So here goes: 'I promise, I vow, I affirm, or anything else you want me to say, that you were born first.' Is that good enough? Satisfied now? You came out of the shell first. I came last. Now give me that food."

Under his breath he mumbled, "You soft-feathered mama baby! What does it matter who came first? Just give me something to eat!"

Hakeber was around the corner and heard every word. She had worried for some time about Emery being so rude and not caring for family traditions, like being proud of having hatched first.

Now she also began to worry about how Jason tricked his brother. He'd really pulled a fast one on Emery this time. By any standard, this had to be a first-class trick. He had taken advantage of Emery's hunger. Yet deep down in her heart, she thought it probably was all right. In fact, she liked the new agreement.

That night when they were settling down to sleep, she thought this was a good time for a little pillow talk with her husband. She nestled close to him and whispered sweetly, "Drake, guess what happened today?"

He moved his wing away from hers and quacked softly, "I know what happened. Emery told me."

"Don't be upset, darling," cooed Hakeber. "Maybe that's how the Great Spirit wanted it in the first place."

"How do you know?" snapped Drake in a voice more sharp than he intended. "I never heard anything about it."

"But I did. Remember those thirty days when I was hatching that egg? Well, I had time to think and to listen. That's when the Great Spirit told me."

"Told you what?" Drake had a touch of irritation in his voice. "Told you that our kids would swap a bowl of grits for a stupid promise?"

"No, not that. And please don't be upset. It's just that the Great Spirit told me that the oldest of the twins would be the strongest, but he would serve the younger one."

"What utter nonsense! You must have heard wrong," quacked Drake. "It's always the other way round. The oldest leads, and the youngest follows. Good night."

He turned his back and went off to sleep. At least he tried to sleep. Clearly he wasn't interested in discussing it further. Drake certainly hadn't accepted what the kids had done. There was nothing binding in careless kitchen talk like that. Nor had he accepted what Hakeber had told him about the Great Spirit's message to her.

One day when all four of them were out for a little walk again, Drake suggested they go for a swim in the pond. The boys raced ahead to the water. Soon they came back as fast as they had gone, shouting, "The water's gone! The pond is dry!"

When Drake and Hakeber got there, they saw it for themselves. There was no pond and no water at all.

"That does it!" announced Drake in a tone that showed he had decided.

"That does what, my dear?" asked his wife.

"We're moving. It hasn't rained all summer, and we'd better clear out of here before worse things happen. Let's go back and start packing."

Hakeber didn't like the idea of moving. She was upset that it was so sudden and Drake hadn't discussed it with her. But she said nothing.

They moved. There wouldn't have been anything unusual about it except that the next day, when they were ready to pull out, Emery was nowhere to be seen. He was simply gone.

Drake became impatient. "Who saw Emery last? Where is he? What is that kid up to?"

Just when Father Drake was about to organize a search party, Emery came waddling across the field. As if nothing was wrong, he sat down beside the family and their baggage. He offered no explanation. No apology.

Turning to Drake, Hakeber asked in a low whisper, "Aren't you going to talk to him? He needs to be disciplined."

"Not now," replied Drake. "Let's just be glad he's here and going along with us."

Hakeber wondered if her husband was blind. Couldn't he see what was going on? Was he afraid of Emery? They had to stop this kind of disrespect for family rules. Jason would never have done a thing like that.

Soon they settled in a new spot where there was plenty of water. Right away, Emery was gone again. This time when he came back, he wasn't alone. With him was a cute chick, a young ducky about his age.

But she was not their kind. When Drake and Hakeber wanted to talk to him about it, Emery laughed and told them to save their breath. He liked her, and they'd better accept her, too. Or else. After all he was of age, wasn't he?

Some time after that sad face-off, Drake and Hakeber were talking, and he was watching her face the way he usually did when they talked. He liked to see her clear-cut features, especially her gentle smile and soft eyes. Drake liked to watch the expressions on his wife's face change as they talked.

He rubbed his eyes and looked at her again. Then he quacked sadly, "I'm afraid my eyes are failing me. I can't see like I used to. Were you smiling or frowning just now?"

"Neither," replied Hakeber. "I was just listening to you. But I, too, have noticed that you can't see so well."

"Perhaps that's a sign that I've lived long enough," quacked Drake in a tired voice. "I think I should ask Emery to come to me so that I can give him that Special Something."

At the mention of that Special Something, all the bells inside Hakeber started ringing at once. She was instantly alert and knew that she had to act fast. If only her husband would not find out. If only Emery wouldn't suspect anything. If only she didn't panic. If only Jason would cooperate. There were so many *ifs*.

Before she had time to make a plan or talk to Jason, she heard Drake call for Emery.

"Ah, there you are, my boy," he greeted him when he stepped into the room. "My eyes are getting weak, and my energy is low. I suppose you've noticed how tired I get. I think I'll die soon.

"But before I die, I want to pass on to you that Special Something that you have coming to you as the one who hatched first. Let's make a celebration of it, shall we?"

"Of course, Father," agreed Emery. "Just say the word, and I'll do whatever you ask."

For a brief moment, the thought crossed his mind to tell his father that he had traded being hatched first with his brother. But then he remembered that his father knew about it and said it didn't mean a thing. No need to bring it up now.

When Drake heard his son say that he would do anything he would ask, he was pleased. It was just like old times. Lately Emery hardly ever shared with him or seemed to care much what the blind old duck did.

"Go out where the grass is deep and where the bugs and beetles are plentiful. Get me a dinner," requested Drake. "Bring me my favorite co-le-OP-tera. That will help make it special. I want it meaningful when I pass the Special Something on to you."

Father Drake heard Emery go away, though he couldn't see him. "Take your time," he called after him.

Emery quacked back, "See you as soon as I catch the coleoptera."

From the next room, Hakeber had heard every word. It was too much for her. This was not how it was to be. The Great Spirit had told her that the youngest, Jason, was to receive that Special Something. Jason didn't fully understand, Emery didn't seem to care, and her husband had paid no attention to what she had told him.

Hakeber believed that the Great Spirit wanted to see things come out right. But now things were going wrong. If Emery came home with those coleoptera, his father would eat them and give him that Special Something. She had to prevent that from happening.

"Jason, come here quickly," she called, as she ran to the kitchen. There she told Jason everything that she had heard. Together they planned how to stop Father Drake from giving the Special Something to Emery, that no-good brother of his. They talked fast, and when they separated and went their own ways, it was clear that they had agreed on a plan of action.

It was just about noon and time for lunch. Hakeber came back into the kitchen. Jason was still there, practicing, trying to quack like his brother Emery.

"I think I've got it." He was cheerful. "Listen to this." He made the usual quacking sounds that ducks make before eating. They sounded almost like Emery's quacks, but not quite. His mother told him to practice a bit more while she put the finishing touches to a dish of grubs mixed with seed mush. She was hoping that her husband's taste was as bad as his sight.

Hakeber gave Jason the dish of food with a friendly smile and an encouraging word. But inside, she was not so sure that the trick would work. It would be terrible if it failed.

"Here's your lunch," quacked Jason, as he stepped up to his almost-blind father. "I hope you enjoy it."

"That didn't take you long," replied Drake. "How come you're be back so soon?"

"The Great Spirit was with me, Father. He led

me straight to the coleoptera." Jason's heart was beating so fast he feared his father would hear it.

"Are these coleoptera that I'm eating?" he asked. "They seem to have a little different taste today."

"Yes, Father, you're eating coleoptera," he lied. The words almost stuck in his throat. But he continued, trying to sound like Emery. "Perhaps they taste a bit different today because of the dry weather lately."

Father Drake finished off the plate and wiped his beak. "Come close to me, Emery, so I can put my wing on your head. This is how it is done in our family when the Special Something is passed on to the next generation. The touch is important. Not that anything actually passes from me to you in the touch, but the Great Spirit does something.

"The words are important, too, for the one giving the Special Something as well as the one receiving it. We both have to believe that the Great Spirit will do what we say."

Father Drake waited a moment as he adjusted his wing carefully on Jason's head. Then he said all those special words about the Great Spirit making him strong, keeping him well, giving him and his wife lots of ducklings, plenty of food, and especially making him the leader of all the ducks in his flock. His brothers and everyone else would bow to him and serve him.

Jason left his father and was in the kitchen telling his mother all about having received the Special Something. They saw Emery come home and go to his father.

Soon they heard Emery tell his father that he had brought the coleoptera for his lunch and was ready to receive the Special Something.

"I've been tricked!" cried Father Drake as if stabbed in the back. "I've been deceived. Your brother, Jason, was here before you, and I gave the Special Something to him. I thought he was you."

Emery was stunned. Suddenly it seemed important that *he* should get that Special Something, not his younger brother. For the first time since he was a duckling, he began to cry.

"Father, oh, my father," he sobbed, "surely you have more than one Special Something. Please give me one, too."

"I'm dreadfully sorry," replied his father. His tone showed that he, too, was shaken to the core by what had happened. "I'm so sorry, Emery, so very sorry. We've been tricked. I gave the Special Something to Jason."

Suddenly Emery's mood changed. He got up and went outside. He was so mad that he almost exploded. He waddled about looking for his brother, Jason. He had only one thing on his mind—find him and kill him.

That's exactly what he would have done if Mother Hakeber hadn't quickly sent Jason away to live with his uncle in another country far away.

What happened to Jason there and how he tricked his uncle—that's another story.

You may compare this story with the one in Genesis 25:21-34 and 27:1-41. The name Hakeber is Rebekah written backward.

"I thought rivalry between brothers or sisters was something learned," wheezed Willi Weasel. "According to the story we just heard, it must have been inherited."

"Probably a bit of both, inherited and developed," muttered Mark Muskrat, his friend. "Either way, it's horrible. Nothing but tension, jealousy, and fights."

"I hear Sonja Squirrel is going to tell us a story this afternoon," Willi noted. "Let's go to hear what she has to say."

Rabbit was up on his podium, the tree trunk, trying to get everyone to settle down. When it was quiet, he announced, "Just look who is with us this afternoon! Our young friend Sonja Squirrel.

"We've had fathers and a mother and even a grandmother tell stories, but this is the first time a youngster is going to tell one. You will soon find out why.

"Sonja, don't worry about the crowd. Just tell us your story. We're all listening."

"The reason they asked me to tell the story," began Sonja, "is because it is about younger animals. Well, not only about them, but the young girls in the story are my age and they are my cousins. So I know who I am talking about.

"I love my cousins. They're good girls. But when we're young, we haven't had much time to learn from experience and become wise. Let me say no more but get on with the story.

"I'm calling it 'The Squirrel Festival,' and you'll soon know why. Wanda and Florence are two of my favorite cousins. Here's the story."

Afternoon: Squirrel's Story

The Squirrel Festival

Wanda held up her long bushy tail. She turned around slowly so all could see it.

"It's . . . wow . . . beautiful!" exclaimed her squirrel friends. They continued brushing and combing their own tails, hoping to make them as lovely as hers.

"Won't the boys go wild when they see us?" squealed one of them.

Another added, "This is going to be the best Squirrel Festival ever."

They were chattering happily when suddenly they remembered that they were not ready for the big event.

Wanda and her four friends knew exactly what had to be done. Sprucing up was only part of the preparation. A more important part was to gather nuts for the banquet.

"Let's go gather nuts right now," suggested Wanda cheerfully. "It's a lovely day, and we don't want to leave things to the last minute."

"A good idea," agreed her friends. They hurried

off into the woods, carrying the baskets between them.

They had been gathering and picking nuts for some time when they came upon Florence and her friends. They were playing hide-and-seek in the bushes, having a great time.

"Hi, Wanda! Hi, girls!" shouted Florence as she passed them, chasing one of her friends. "Why don't you join us in the fun?"

"No thanks," replied Wanda. "We have work to do. We're going to the annual Squirrel Festival. We have to get ready."

"We're going, too," Florence yelled, "but there's lots of time to get ready. Come on, don't be a spoilsport. Stay here and play with us. Just for a little while."

Wanda and her friends moved into a huddle for a quick discussion. In less than a minute, they were ready with their answer.

"No thanks. We'd love to, but we really don't have time. The Squirrel Festival is next week, and we want to be sure we're ready. We wouldn't want to miss that fun for anything."

"Have it your way," chattered Florence. "We're going to have fun now *and* at the festival." With that she dashed up a large maple and hid in the branches. Soon her friends followed her, and Wanda heard happy squealing and laughter coming from the top of the trees.

Then came the day to start on the long trip to the Squirrel Festival. Wanda and her friends were ready. They had gathered enough nuts for food on the trip and for the days of celebration. She was thinking about Florence and her friends, wondering whether they were ready, when they came around the corner.

"What a happy happening," called Florence. "You don't mind if we join you?"

"Not at all," responded Wanda. "We're delighted to have you join us. If it's anything like other years, there are going to be a lot of squirrels going up with us to the festival."

They walked on together, all moving in the same direction. Everyone was excited and expecting a great time. As they met more squirrels, they greeted each other cheerfully.

All of them carried bags or baskets of nuts. All of them, that is, except Florence and her fun-loving friends. They had their baskets along, but they didn't have many nuts in them. They planned to gather them along the way.

That's exactly what they did. Whenever they got hungry, they simply dashed off into a nearby woods and found a few nuts or acorns for a quick lunch. They thought they were rather smart, doing it that way.

In the first place, it was fun. In the second place, they didn't have to carry the heavy baskets filled with nuts like the others. Florence and her friends didn't seem to have a worry in the world.

Not a worry in the world, that is, until suddenly they realized that they were almost at the festival. They knew that every squirrel was expected to bring nuts to the great Squirrel Festival.

This year was going to be especially exciting because the King of Squirrel Land was going to be there. They didn't want to miss seeing him. They had even been told that they would all be seated at the same banquet table with him. But not if they hadn't brought their basket of nuts along.

"Now watch me," bragged Florence to her friends. "We need nuts, and I'm going to get nuts!"

In two or three masterful leaps, she was beside her friend and fellow traveler Wanda. Florence smiled broadly at Cousin Wanda and began her pitch.

"Wanda, dear, we've had a bit of bad luck. We meant to gather nuts along the way, but we only found enough for our lunches. We need nuts for the banquet. Your baskets are so full. I'm sure you and your friends won't mind sharing with us. Would you?"

When she saw the expression on Wanda's face, she quickly added, "I don't mean *giving* us nuts. We just want to borrow some. As soon as we get home, we'll pay you back right away."

Wanda looked carefully at her basket of nuts and at the nearly empty baskets of Florence and her friends. She was sorry for them, but then she said, "Normally I'd be happy to share with you, Florence, but you know how long the festival lasts.

"If we give you half of ours, you still won't have enough to last to the end of the festival, and there won't be enough left for us, either. I'm terribly sorry. There just aren't enough for all of us. Why don't you run and quickly try to find some more? You have a bit of time left."

"Come on, girls!" Florence called to her friends.

"Let's go and find us some nuts."

They dashed off into a woods not far away. The gathering was not as good as they had expected. They found a few, but not nearly enough to last them through the days of celebration. They raced up the trees and just as quickly came down again—nothing.

They searched on the ground, but couldn't find any nuts there either, not even acorns. They pushed the leaves on the ground this way and that, hoping there would be nuts under them, but there were none.

"What are we going to do?" whined one of the squirrels almost in tears. "Look, our baskets are still almost empty!"

"Don't worry." Florence tried to use a calm voice. "Everything is going to be all right. We just have to find the right trees, that's all. When we find them, we'll fill our baskets in no time."

Florence and her friends hunted for over an hour, but their baskets remained nearly empty. They knew they had to hurry and fill them because soon they would hear the trumpet announcing the start of the Squirrel Festival. That would also mean the gates would be closed, and nobody would be allowed to go in after that.

"I wish we had gotten ready like the others," groaned one of the squirrels. "Then this wouldn't have happened to us."

"I think we were foolish when we were just having fun," whimpered another unhappily. "We should have gathered nuts like Wanda and her friends did."

"Now cut that out!" snapped Florence in an angry tone of voice. "All that moaning and groaning isn't going to fill our baskets. But this isn't the end of the world. Just come along and watch me solve this little problem."

With that, Florence turned in the direction of another little forest. "Come on girls, run!" she encouraged them. "Look what I found!" Sure enough, there were nuts galore. The girls gathered them up as quickly as possible. Soon their baskets were filled.

"There now, didn't I tell you?" squealed Florence. "We did it. Now let's hurry to the festival."

They were running as fast as they could when they heard shouts in the distance. Then the noise got louder. Florence and her friends knew what that meant: the King of Squirrel Land had arrived. Those were the shouts and the cheers of welcome. They ran faster and faster.

They had almost reached the main gate leading into the Squirrel Festival grounds when they heard a trumpet sound. It was long and loud. The cheers and noise inside increased. Then there were three more short blasts on the trumpet.

Suddenly it was silent. There was a great stillness all around. Not long after that, Florence and her friends reached the gate. It was closed.

For a moment they stood outside, just catching their breath from running so fast. One of the squirrels began to cry. Florence knocked on the gate. There was no response.

She knocked louder. Then she called to the gatekeeper, "Open up, please. We've come to the festival. We're here for the banquet with the king!"

At last they heard someone on the inside. For a moment, they were hopeful again. Florence chattered once more, "Open up, please. We have come to the Squirrel Festival. We have come to the banquet with the King of Squirrel Land!"

There was a moment of silence. Then a voice came from the inside: "It is too late. The banquet has started, and we cannot interrupt it. Go away!"

Florence wanted to say something, but she didn't know what. Her friends were crying. Between their sobs and tears, she heard one of them moaning over and over again, "We came too late! Too late!"

Jesus told this story, just a little differently, and his disciple Matthew wrote it down in his Gospel, 25:1-13.

"Now wasn't that a wonderful story!" chattered Charlie Chipmunk. "Too bad they didn't get to the festival. But I bet they learned their lesson."

"If you ask me," rattled Rony Raccoon, "preparation is everything! That's why I read books and go to school. I want to be ready for the things of life when I get older."

"By the way, the story tonight is about your uncle, isn't it?"

"That's right. Uncle Alex. Most of us called him Alex Coony. He was lots of fun and quite smart. But he still got into trouble, maybe because he was cocky, so sure he was so smart."

Both boys heard the bell. It was time for the last story. To their surprise, Felix Fox was going to tell it.

"This is our final gathering," began Chairman Rabbit. "I hope you all enjoyed it. As you know, the storytellers are all volunteers. Their stories are true, and we are most grateful to them for sharing their tales with us.

"This is not a competition. We give no prizes and no awards. And that's how we want to keep it if we have another Storytime Jamboree."

The animals gave loud and long applause, whistling and shouting, "Encore! Encore!" Finally they all got up while they continued clapping their paws. When at last they sat down again on the grass, Rabbit continued.

"Now we'll hear one more story, and our jamboree will be history. Tonight's story is about a clever but not very honest raccoon. He's dead now, but Felix Fox knew him well.

"I happen to know that Foxy and Coony, if I may call them that, were good friends. So, Foxy, tell us about your friend. You have a reputation for being clever yourself. Did you ever match wits with Coony?"

"Whether Alex Raccoon was more clever than I, is not for me to say," replied Fox. "But, yes, he was my good friend, and I hope you all learn a lesson from him. Maybe two lessons, because my story about Alex is really in two parts. I'm going to call it, 'Coony, You're a Loony.' "

Evening: Fox's Story

Coony, You're a Loony

Alex thought that, among all the raccoons, none were as clever as he. With his stout body and short legs, he was able to go almost anywhere he chose—grubbing in the vegetable garden, climbing fruit trees, swimming in the nearby lake, and even scaling the roof of the farmer's house.

Most of Coony's friends and cousins had five black rings on their tails. A few had six. Alex was the only one who had seven rings on his tail. This helped him keep track of the days in the week.

He was especially proud of his slender forefeet. They were small and delicate. When he secretly watched the farmer at work and compared the farmer's hands with his own, Alex could see little difference. He even thought there weren't many things that the farmer did with his hands that he couldn't do with his, also.

Most of all, Alex was proud of his high intelligence. He didn't know another animal—even me, his best friend, Felix Fox—as cunning as he. That was why he could live such a good life, he thought.

All his cousins and other coons of the community worked hard to get enough food for themselves, but Alex had his food brought to him. He had a way with everybody that always worked in his favor. Whether he ordered frogs or berries, eggs or fruit, they always delivered a bountiful supply.

In one thing Alex Coony was just like all other coons: he loved fresh corn picked straight off the stalk. He could hardly wait for late summer, when the cobs would be tender and juicy, just right for one feast after another.

Like all coons, he avoided being seen in the daytime. He feasted at night. The other coons brought him as much as he demanded because they all knew that he was the official food collector for Lotor, the Chief of Racoon Land.

Lotor, meaning "washer," was famous for always washing his food before he ate it, as an example to the other coons.

For his pay, Alex was allowed to keep one part out of twenty. He was able to figure this out on his toes, five on each of his four paws.

One day a rumor got out that Alex was not honest. The whispering went to one ear after the other that he was cheating Lotor, the chief.

Instead of turning over to him the amount of food agreed upon, so the whisper had it, Alex always kept back too much for himself. Somebody must have noticed that the pile collected from the coons was much bigger than the pile turned over to the chief.

Soon the other coons put two and two together. The gossip continued to spread like wildfire that Alex was so pudgy and roly-poly because he stuffed himself with food collected for Chief Lotor but not delivered to him. Alex always kept back a lot for himself, more like two parts out of twenty.

One day Alex was just enjoying another juicy corncob when there was a sharp knock on his door.

"Come in," he called out cheerfully. "Come in and have a cob."

"No thanks," replied the visitor. "I have a message for you. Chief Lotor wants to see you."

The smile was gone from Alex's face even before he could wipe away the dripping juice. He jumped up, looked this way and that with worry in his eyes, and finally said he'd be there just as soon as he could.

"That's not good enough," stated the messenger. "I have orders to bring you along with me *right now.*"

Alex panicked. He knew why Lotor wanted to see him. His head reeled, and his mind whirled. What should he do? What could he say?

Suddenly he felt sick in his stomach and knew it wasn't from the corn. Oh, why haven't I been honest! he groaned inside.

"Let's go!" ordered the messenger. "Chief Lotor is waiting."

Poor Alex! He had no choice but to go along. He felt that a tree was falling on his life. This was it! He'd be smashed, fired, put out of a rewarding job.

"What's this I hear about you stealing from me?" demanded Chief Lotor when Alex stood facing him. "You're really stealing from the people. Is it true that you always collect more than you are supposed to and keep too much for yourself?"

The charge was true; he was cheating, and he could not deny it. Alex Coony fully expected to be pushed into a hunter's trap and have his leg caught there.

He was trembling and stuttering nonsense when Chief Lotor ordered, "Tomorrow you bring me *all* of what you have collected from the community. Then you're fired.

"I will not have a collector working for me who is not honest. *Now get out!*"

Alex was relieved, but also worried. Relieved that he would not have his leg clamped in a trap, but worried about his future. Now what should he do? His fat job was over.

That meant Alex would have to get out and work like all the other coons. But he wasn't used to working. He'd gotten so chubby because he was such a clever middleman.

For a little while, everything seemed dark for Alex. Then he an idea. Being who he was, he thought it was a brilliant idea. Quick as a flash, he tried it.

"You owe me some frogs for Lotor's kitchen," he announced to one of the coons. "Do you remember how many? The chief wants me to deliver them tomorrow."

"I owe seven frogs," replied that coon, just a bit frightened at the sudden notice. "I don't know whether I can catch seven by tomorrow. Isn't there anything you can do to help?"

"You happen to be talking to the right coon," replied Alex with a broad smile. "I'm your friend. Be sure to remember that. Now forget about the seven frogs. Just get me four. I'll tell Lotor you only owed him four."

Moments later, Alex was at the next house talking to another coon about the number of melons he owed Chief Lotor.

"The order is . . . ah . . . for three melons," stammered the startled coon. "But you say I am to deliver them tomorrow? I can't do that. Not that soon. Please help me. I'm in deep trouble."

"Don't worry." Alex was grinning from ear to ear. "I know how to fix this. But mind you, this is just between you and me. Nobody must find out about it. Strike out that you owe three big melons. Just get me one, and it doesn't have to be big."

"You are my friend," responded the coon gratefully. "I'll never forget that. Any time you need help, just come to me."

The scheme was working. Once again Alex was proving that he was a smart coony. He would be out of a job, but he had nothing to worry about. His friends would take care of him.

They would actually think they owed it to him. Just to make sure he was well taken care of, he continued his racket a bit longer.

"And how are you this morning?" he asked a poor widow whose husband had died in a trap not long ago.

"Fair. Just middling," she replied. "I'm alone now and also getting older. It takes me a long time to get things done."

"That's too bad," soothed Alex Coony, pretending to be sorry for her. "And on top of that, you have to deliver corn to the chief. It's six cobs, isn't it?"

"It is," replied the widow. "But how am I going to get the six cobs, at my age, with this arthritis?"

"There now, Grandma, don't you worry," Alex soothed her. "I'm sure we can work something out. Now suppose we say you owe Chief Lotor two cobs, not six. How would you like that?"

"Why, that would be wonderful!" exclaimed the widow. "I think I could manage that."

"Well then, it's settled," stated Alex. "Just deliver two cobs."

Widow Coon was so happy she almost hugged Alex. "You're a real friend! I'll never forget what you did for me."

Alex smiled and was about to leave when she called after him, "Come for dinner anytime. You're always welcome!"

When Chief Lotor heard what Alex had done, he declared, "He's a rascal! A dishonest but clever rascal! That coon is a loon.

"I don't want anyone to follow his example. But on the other hand, I can't help admiring him. Why aren't there more coons in my community as smart as Alex, but a bit more honest?"

• • •

Once, before all this happened and before Alex had gotten fired, Lotor, Chief of the Raccoons, had all his food collectors come together for an accounting. What Chief Lotor wanted to know was how much each one of these collectors owed him. This is how the system worked.

In each town and village and for each country area, there were food collectors. They gathered food from everyone in the community and delivered it to Chief Lotor. He needed that for himself, his family, and all the coons that worked for him. Each collector was to keep one part out of twenty for wages.

Everything was going just fine until it was Alex's turn to step forward and explain his situation. Poor Alex! He'd been at it again, cheating and skimming off too much food for himself.

He thought he was so clever that he could get away with it. But now he was in trouble. The more questions Chief Lotor asked, the less Alex was able to answer. Chief Lotor finally summed it up.

"It seems to me you owe quite a pile, Alex. If our figures are correct, it is over a hundred food items. What do you say to that?"

Alex admitted that the figures were correct. But he did not have the goods to deliver. Alex was so frantic that he did something he had never done before. He fell down on his knees in front of Chief Lotor, whimpered like a puppy, and begged for time.

"Please, sir, don't put me in jail," he begged. "Please don't take my wife and children away from me. All I need is a little time. Please give me time, and I'll bring you everything I owe."

Chief Lotor looked down on Alex, worried, lying at his feet, crying and begging for time. He felt sorry for the poor coon.

"Stand on your feet!" ordered Lotor. "I have a surprise for you. Look at me."

When Alex stood up and looked Lotor in the face, he saw a warm smile there instead of the cold stare he had expected. He could hardly believe his ears when he heard Chief Lotor say, "Coon Alex, you don't owe me anything! I cancel all your debt. Go in peace."

Alex walked on air the rest of that morning. There was a song in his heart. "No debts! All canceled! I'm free!" He was so happy! Life was good. Lotor was good.

About two o'clock that afternoon in the poor section of town, Alex happened to meet a coon who owed him three eggs. Right away, he put his claws into the coon's fur about his debt and told him to pay up.

"Look at it this way," he growled in a cold voice. "You should have seen the trouble I was in this morning. I was scared to death. All because little guys like you haven't paid up.

"If you had paid me the way you are supposed to, I could have paid my debt. So come on, shell out! Pay up or else!"

"Be reasonable," pleaded the coon. "How can I pay you now? I barely have enough to feed my children today. You have to give me a little time. Not much, just a few days. I'll pay you, for sure."

"You miserable liar," snarled Alex, reaching for his throat. "You no-good cheat! So it's time you want, is it? Well, I'll see that you get time. In jail you'll have plenty of time to think about what you should have done. It's too late now! Come along."

Alex pulled the poor coon along, calling for the police to arrest him and throw him in prison. Other coons were watching in amazement. They could hardly believe what they saw. One of them ran off to tell Chief Lotor.

When Lotor heard this, he sent for Alex a second time. Even from a distance, Alex could tell that the chief's face no longer had that smile and kindly look. He was stern and serious.

For a while Chief Lotor said nothing, he was so angry. Finally he spoke. "You selfish and evil coon! You cold and heartless creature! Only a few hours ago, you lay in front of me whining for time. I gave you more than time. I canceled all your debts. Over a hundred food items, if I remember correctly.

"Now when a poor coon brother asks you to give him time to pay you back the three eggs he owes, you have him thrown into prison!"

Chief Lotor got up, looked down on Alex cowering at his feet, and ordered, "Take him away and lock him up in prison. Don't let him out until he's paid every one of the hundred pieces that he owes."

As they led Alex away to prison, Chief Lotor explained to those around him, "Why should I have pity on him? He didn't have pity on the little guy. Serves him right!"

Jesus told these two stories, only a bit differently. You will find them in Luke 16:1-13 and Matthew 18:23-35.

**Chief Lotor ordered,
"Take Alex away and lock him up."**

Bedtime: Beaver's Good-Bye

Questions

"There he is! Get him! Bring him here!" shouted the youngsters after the last meeting of the jamboree.

A number of the faster ones raced off to get Beaver to join them one more time for a final informal get-together.

"Okay, I'll tell you a short story." Beaver laughed. "Or perhaps after all these stories, you have questions."

"Yes, we do," chattered Charlie Chipmunk. "Especially about the Great Spirit. So many of the stories mentioned the Great Spirit. Can you tell us a bit more about him?"

"I'll try. One thing we know for sure—he loves youngsters. Once, long ago, the Son of the Great Spirit came to live among us for a while and showed us what the Great Spirit was like.

"When this Son heard that there was some child abuse, he became angry. He said that anyone who hurt a little one should be drowned in a deep pond, with a stone around his neck.

"Now, whether those are the exact words the Son used, I don't know. But he sure let them know that he wasn't going to stand still for any messing around with children.

"One time a little girl died, the only child in her family. Her parents were terribly sad. So the Son of the Great Spirit bent over her and brought her back to life again. And guess what he told the parents?"

"To take better care of her next time?" suggested Sammy Squirrel.

"That they should be thankful?" volunteered Robin Raccoon.

"Those are good answers," responded Beaver, "but that's not what he said. He told the parents to get her something to eat.

"Talking about food—another time there were thousands of animals without food. The Son of the Great Spirit did a great honor to a little fellow who came and offered him his lunch.

"The Son accepted it and didn't say anything about it not being enough to feed so many. He smiled at the youth and thanked him kindly. Then he asked the Great Spirit to make the meal good, broke the food into pieces, and had it passed out to the crowd.

"Well, you might know the rest of this famous story. Everybody got enough to eat, and there was some left over. Don't ask me how he did it. The point is that it happened, and he allowed a youngster to be his helper.

"Another time there was a great crowd, almost like at this jamboree. Some mothers came with their little ones to get the Special Something for them. The older animals chased them away, saying the Son of the Great Spirit had more important things to do.

But he heard the commotion and called to them, "Don't drive them away. I love the little ones. Bring them to me." He played with them, stroked them, held them, and talked with them. Finally he gave them the "Special Something."

"Oh, yes, he loves the little ones. He loves the children. He loves you. Surely he was with us at this Storytime Jamboree."

The young animals had one more question. "Will we have another jamboree like this next year?"

"I hope so, and we will plan for it," Beaver assured them. "There are so many more stories that we should share with each other.

"Don't forget to ask your parents at home to tell you their stories. Each family has some. Don't lose them! They are the best things your parents can give you. Ask them to tell you stories about their experiences, and stories about the Great Spirit."

"Now it is time for you to run on home and get some sleep. See you at our next jamboree!"

For the originals of these stories, see Matthew 18:5-6; Luke 8:49-55; John 6:6-14; and Matthew 19:13-15.

The Author

Peter J. Dyck was born in Russia and came to Canada with his family at age twelve. He settled in Saskatchewan. After high school, he attended the University of Saskatchewan, Goshen College, Bethel College, and Mennonite Biblical and Bethany Theological seminaries.

For some years, he served as pastor near Sudbury, Ontario; at Moundridge, Kansas; and at Scottdale, Pennsylvania. He also taught at the Bienenberg Bible School in Switzerland.

In 1941, Peter volunteered to help war victims in England, where he met and married Elfrieda Klassen. After World War II, they did relief work in Holland and helped Mennonite refugees move from Russia to North and South America. In their book, *Up from the Rubble*, they show pictures and tell exciting stories about their adventures during this period.

Peter and Elfrieda have worked with the Mennonite Central Committee for more than thirty years. Peter's book *A Leap of Faith* shows how MCC helps people who are in trouble.

Now the Dycks live at Akron, Pennsylvania, where they are members of the Akron Mennonite Church. Their two daughters and five grandchildren tested the earlier stories, *A Leap of Faith* and the two *Shalom* books, and said they liked them. We hope they and all of you will like these *Jamboree* stories, too. Peter is now in active retirement, with many speaking appointments.